THE

Gospel

TRUTH

THE

Gospel

TRUTH

Caroline Pignat

Red Deer Press

Published in Canada by Red Deer Press, 195 Allstate Parkway, Markham, Ontario L3R 4T8
Published in the United States by Red Deer Press, 311 Washington Street, Brighton, Massachusetts 02135

www.reddeerpress.com

10 9 8 7 6 5 4 3 2

Red Deer Press acknowledges with thanks the Canada Council for the Arts, and the Ontario Arts Council for their support of our publishing program. We acknowledge the financial support of the Government of Canada through the Canada Book Fund (CBF) for our publishing activities.

Canada Council for the Arts **Conseil des Arts du Canada**

ONTARIO ARTS COUNCIL
CONSEIL DES ARTS DE L'ONTARIO
an Ontario government agency
un organisme du gouvernement de l'Ontario

Library and Archives Canada Cataloguing in Publication
Pignat, Caroline, author
The gospel truth / Caroline Pignat.
Issued in print and electronic formats.
ISBN 978-0-88995-493-9 (pbk.).--ISBN 978-1-55244-349-1 (pdf)
1. Underground Railroad--Juvenile fiction. I. Title.
PS8631.I4777G67 2014   jC813'.6   C2014-904728-2
C2014-904729-0

Publisher Cataloging-in-Publication Data (U.S.)
Pignat, Caroline.
The gospel truth / Caroline Pignat.
[328] pages : cm.
Summary: Phoebe is a 16 year old slave girl living on a Virginia plantation in the 1850s, when the plantation is visited by an abolitionist who poses as a birdwatcher. This character is based on the real-life Alexander Milton Ross, a.k.a. the Birdman. Knowing the harsh realities of life on the plantation, Phoebe comes to realize that she has a chance to risk escape along the route of the Underground Railroad. Phoebe's story is a compelling tribute to the hundreds of African Americans who made this journey.
ISBN-13: 978-0-88995-493-9 (pbk.)
Also published in electronic formats.
1. Child slaves – United States – Juvenile fiction. 2. Underground railroad – Juvenile fiction. 3. Slavery – United States – Juvenile fiction. 4. Ross, Alexander Milton, 1832-1897 – Juvenile fiction. I. Title.
[Fic] dc23   PZ7.P4353Go 2014

Edited for the Press by Peter Carver
Cover design by Alan Cranny
Cover image courtesy of Alan Cranny
Text design by Daniel Choi
Printed in Canada by Friesens Corporation

MIX
Paper from
responsible sources
FSC® C016245
www.fsc.org

For Peter—who helps so many of us find our voices.

Whitehaven Plantation
Virginia, 1858

Yellow Bird

I thought it was done for, that bright yellow bird
flap-fluttering as Rufus closed his jaws,
'til it lie,
                limp
beneath his whiskers.

I clap and run at Rufus
and that old scaredy-cat
drop it and bolt under the porch
where he sit whipping his tail,
watching me kneel over his prey:
                a splash of yellow on the wet green,
                head tilted,
                wing splayed
                and dotted with blood red beads.

It look dead.

But I lift it in my cupped hands,
and I know it ain't.

I feel it—
that tiny heart tap-tapping, strong and true.

It feel like hope.

Two Truths

Its right wing hangs loose from its shoulder
like a tattered shawl of yellow.
"Can you fix it?" Miss Tessa ask me
as Rufus rub himself around her skirts.

I don't rightly know.

"Fetch the birdcage from the attic," she say.
So I do.
And I put the trembling bird inside.
It hobble and hunch in the corner
as I fill the small dishes with water and seed.
But that yellow bird don't drink
or eat.
She just go real still.

"Is it dead, Phoebe?" Miss Tessa ask.
I shake my head.
That bird just so scared of what is,
it gotta go on pretending what isn't.

Acting dead in the bottom of its cage
so as it don't end up that way.
That's hope, that is.
Only not the kind of hope Miss Tessa ever know.

Yellow feathers tremble in the corner,
make my heart ache with truth:
>   it don't wanna be in here.
>   No bird belong behind bars.

Rufus slink over,
rub against my leg,
lick his black lips with that gritty pink tongue
and my head know another truth:

sometimes the safest place to be is
in a cage.

The Way of Things

Master call us out to the yard,
make everyone gather round as Brutus ride in,
big Will stumbling behind him,
hands tied,
clothes torn,
his many muscles shiny black with sweat and blood.

Brutus lead him by a rope around his neck,
like some old hound.
He pull Will over and kick him down before
Master standing on the porch.
And big Will, the biggest slave I ever seen,
don't look so big no more.

I's happy to see Will alive.
And sad to see Will here.

"You think you can run from me, boy?" Master say,
walking his polished boots down the steps.
"Trying to run—why, that's like trying to steal from me."

Master tap his riding crop in his hand as he circle
Will kneeling in the dirt,
"And *nobody* steals from Arnold Duncan."
He swing that crop, cutting Will's cheek.
Once. Twice. Three times.

Will spit blood in the sand.

"Peel and pickle him," Master say to Brutus.
Shad gasp beside me.
Will is his older brother, the only family he got left.

When a slave's back be all peeled by the whip
and pickled by buckets of saltwater,
just to make it sting even more,
some slaves die from a whipping like that.
And some just die inside.

Master go back into the Big House
with Missus and Miss Tessa
as Brutus take out a knife,
cut off what ragged clothes Will got left.
He turn him round
and tie Will's thick arms around the post.
The whip snap,
and we all jump like it hitting us.
In some way, it is.
Big Will bleeding
but we all be scarred.

And nobody ever gonna think of running again.
Crack! Crack! Crack!

I grip Shad's hand.
Forty-nine. Fifty.
Brutus stop for a rest, chest heaving.
Wipe his sweaty white forehead on his dirty sleeve.
Then gets back to work.

Two hundred strokes he give
while Will grunt, groan, and grit his teeth,
trying not to cry out.

But his back weeping for all of us.

And nobody does nothing but watch
bloody tears fall in the sand.

Will belong to Master Duncan.
We all do.

It's just the way of things.

Training

Will could get me top dollar at auction.
$1300, at least.

But I don't want to sell him.

Still, I won't brand him with the runaway "R"
much as I'd like to sear it on his skin.
Why let the buyer know he's trouble?
It brings down the value, I say.

Maybe Brutus can break him this time.
But I doubt it.
Will has been a headstrong Negro,
a problem since the day I bought him
and his scrawny brother.
And no amount of whipping,
or starving,
or days in the stocks
seem to help.

My father always said:
There are no bad dogs, just bad owners.
Will is just a Negro.
He can be trained, and tamed, and gentled.
Just like any animal.
With the right amount of
                    … coercion.
I'll do whatever it takes,
Will is that valuable to me.

I don't want to sell him.
I want to break him.
And then—
I want to breed him.

Hush, Now

I never know'd my age.
Bea say I's a year younger than Miss Tessa
—but numbers don't matter none,
except maybe to Master Duncan.
He always be counting something.
Days. Dollars. Slaves.
Marking in his red leather book each night.
I s'pose one of them scribbles is me.

Another is my mother.

I wish I'd known what day it was that he planned to
scratch her out,
to move her name to another man's ledger.
Maybe I could have done something.
Maybe I could have stopped him somehow.
Or at least asked him to move my name, too.

But I's only small then.
How was I to know

that when she kiss me goodbye that morning
before she went to bring Missus her tea,

that that be the last time I'd see her?

I cried for her all winter,
no matter how Bea held me in her big strong arms.
"Hush, now, Phoebe," she whisper in my ear.
"You be a good girl—and, God willing,
you going see your momma someday."

So I hush.

I stop crying.
Stop talking.
I never makes a peep no more.
But I haven't seen my mother in ten summers.
I don't even know if she alive or dead.

Some days, I wonder if I is.

Shad and Bea

It don't matter that I don't talk.
Bea gots enough to say for all of us.
Even as she fly about the kitchen, circling from pot to pan,
she a-buzzing over all she gotta do,
what with Master's guest arriving next week.
"He's some kind of doctor," she say,
"come to see Virginian birds."
I never heard of no bird doctor before.

Bea a real hornet's nest.
Only a fool be the stick that poke her.
In come Shad
splish-splashing the milk buckets he carrying,
and I shakes my head.
Shad be that stick, if I ever saw one—
all long and lean,
ready to stir things up.

"Boy, I swear you going to be the death of me."
Bea cuffs the backside of his head.

"Look at all that milk you wasting!"

Shad set the buckets on the table and rub his thick skull,
his devil's grin tickling his mouth as he watches Rufus
come in and set to licking the spill.
"Bea," he say, "way I see it, I done you a favor:
>I gots you milk
>I fed your cat
>and I washed your floor."

Bea swing at him again, but she aiming to miss.
Me and Shad, we know she's laughing
on the inside.

Bea do all her laughing on the inside.

Shad take a piece of cornbread I's cutting from the pile,
leans on the counter.
"I 'spect my lunch at noon, Miss Beatrice," he say,
like he the Master himself.
He smile at me then.
"Unless Phoebe don't want me to come around, that is."
He waits and looks at me with them eyes,
like two dark pools.
My face feel like I stuck it over the steam,
but the kettle ain't even whistling yet.

Bea shove him out the door.
"Go on and stop your lazing about,

else I get Brutus after you."

Shad get to moving then.

Ain't nobody want Brutus's attention.

And if Bea bring up his name, she ain't laughing no more.

She mean business.

What I Can Do

I can do a lot of things,
  climb any tree,
  whittle a fishing spear,
    turn it into a fishing pole
    —when it don't work,
    and then a sword
    —when the pole don't work neither.
    (Fish too bony, anyhow.)

I can beat Charlie in a duel
  or a race
  or a spitting contest,
  'til he cramp from trying
  or laughing too hard.

I can swim—but not in swamp water.
  Nobody can do that.

I can hit ol' Rufus ten feet away
from both barrels of the cow's udder.

I can pat juba, clap-slapping a beat
that make everyone's feet tap on Saturday night.
I can juggle three biscuits
      (and eats them all, too,
      if you's dumb enough to give me yours).

And I can even make Phoebe smile.

Nobody else know how to do that.
      And that just fine.
      'Cause that's my job.

But there's one thing I can never do.

Understand Will.
      Why he run?
      Why he wanna rile Master?

      Most of all,
            why he leave me?

Miss Tessa's Reading Lesson

I help Bea in the kitchen and I takes care of Miss Tessa.
Miss Tessa, she seventeen,
she old enough to do most things herself,
but she always wanting me doing them for her.
      Comb her hair.
      Lay out her clothes.
      Fetch her lemonade.
I make sure Miss Tessa dress nice and eat proper.
And when she don't have some job for me,
I wait in the corner until she do.

I can disappear like a tree in a forest.
Stand so still and quiet-like,
even a chickadee might land on my head
and get to nesting.

When Mr. Cooke, her tutor, come by
on Tuesdays and Thursdays,
I stand by her side and wave the big feather fan
to keep them cool.

If it weren't for that whisper of wind,
I'd say they'd never even know I was there.

Miss Tessa always do what Miss Tessa want.
And none of them other tutors is smart enough
to make her want to learn.
She never going to read, they say.
But you can't never say never to Missus.
So she hire Mr. Cooke right out of college last spring,
paid him double his teacher's salary to tutor Miss Tessa
if he could have her reading by the harvest.

For weeks now,
Miss Tessa bat her big blue eyes,
ask him to go over it one more time.
Mr. Cooke, he sit right next to her
and run his finger slow-like under the words.
       "Ahhhh," he go.
          "Ahhh," she say.
     "Oooooo," he go.
         "Oooooo," she say,
         her pink lips all puckered up near his.
Sitting right up close with no air between them—

No wonder they's getting all hot.

Lessons Learned

I know'd Miss Tessa better than anyone.
She ain't no fool.
There is a lot going on behind them big blue eyes.
You ask me,
she know how to read.
But Miss Tessa also know how to get what she want—
and she want young Mr. Cooke's attention.
She like the way he lean in beside her.
And he like his paychecks.

And I like how we all keep it secret.

'Cause if anybody know
I learned how to read by listening to him
and that I practice my letters
on her old speller that she throw away,
the one I keep in my hollow tree—

Brutus be teaching me a new lesson.
And that's one I surely don't want to learn.

I f

If Miss Tessa gonna throw out that speller,
maybe I'll just take it.
If Mr. Cooke gonna dish out his lessons,
maybe I'll just learn it.
And if Master Duncan ever leave out
that big red leather book,
maybe I'll just read it.

'Cause if I do,
Maybe, just maybe,

I can find out where Momma been sent.

Taste of Home

A week now, I been watching Yellowbird
wasting away
in her cage in the corner of the dining room.
I know she hungry.
But not for what seed be in them little dishes.

So I go out to the woods to where I seen some yellow birds.
And when I's still enough,
bright ones just like her
flit-flutter from limb to log,
their yellow heads cocked as they skip-hop,
pick, pick, and peck.

Prize wriggling in their beaks,
they swoop back to the honeysuckle
where hidden nestlings calling out,
the ones that can't feed theyselves yet, I s'pose.
I peel a strip of bark off that rotted log,
pick my own tiny caterpillar from its wet underside,
and run to the Big House

as it curl and wriggle in my fingers.
I gots my own bird to feed.

And when I put it in the cage,
Yellowbird turn her black bead eye from me—
from what she fear—
to what she want.
Dragging her limp wing,
she skip-hop over to pick-peck that bug.

I smile.

Shad spying on me from the kitchen door.
He smile, too.

"All it needed was a taste of home," he say.
He think about something for a moment.
"Phoebe," he say, "for a girl, you real smart."

But I ain't.
Any fool can watch and learn
like I do.

The birds,
they's the smart ones.

Curing Barn

I slide the lock on the barn door.
Come harvest, all the tobacco leaves get cured,
dried by fires, in here.
Ghosts of woodsmoke and tobacco
still haunt and whisper in the rafters.

But the barn empty now.
Except for Will.

He lying on his stomach in the corner,
ankles in chains,
flies buzzing at where his back soaked through his shirt.
Like he dead already.
Like he gonna be if he don't smarten up.

I get him a scoop of water from the bucket in the corner.
Pour it in his mouth.
Pour another on his fevered face.
He been in here a week now.
And by my reckoning,

if he be testing his will against Master's,
he losing.
Any fool can see that.
Why can't Will?

"Come on now," I say, putting the cornbread in his hand.
"You gotta eat."

He slowly push himself up,
sit kinda side-like,
gritting his teeth, breathing funny.

"Why you wanna run?" I ask.
He look at me. "Why you wanna stay?"

Will and me, we so different,
sometimes I can't believe we brothers.

"I remember life before Whitehaven." He take a small bite.
"I seen a world outside them fences.
You young," he say.
"You don't know no different, no better."

"I's old enough to know a fool when I see one," I say.
"Why can't you just heed Master?"

Will look at me. "I gots my own mind. My own wants."

"Well, so do I, Will.

How you think I got working in the Big House?"
I smile.
"Someday, I gonna be the butler,
running the place, like old Samuel."

Will shake his head.
"Shad, you can lick Master's boots all you want,
but they still kick you.
They still crush you under their heel."

"You don't know!" I shout. "I got plans.
For me. For Phoebe.
What you got, brother?
Nothing. That's what. Nothing ... but scars."
I so angry, I's shaking.

I snatch the cornbread outta his hand.
"Get your own damn bread if you's so smart."
I slam the door
and slide the crossbar.

Master right.
Will need time in here to do some more thinking.
I just hope the curing barn
can cure the madness in my big brother.

Else I won't have one for much longer.

Healing

Yellowbird like beetles and leafhoppers,
but I know she like juicy caterpillars the best.
Today I put one on her perch. Make her work for it.
I can tell it pain her some, but she do it.
Both wings flapping, she jump
right up on that perch
to snatch where that worm inch along.
Miss Tessa laugh and clap her hands
like it a trick especially for her.
I line the cage with honeysuckle leaves
from the bush where yellow birds nest.
Every day she getting stronger.

"Why won't it sing?" Miss Tessa ask.

I shrug.
Why would she?

Yes, she gonna be all right, Yellowbird.
Like Bea say: *Time heals.*

A week for a wing.
But how long does it take to fix

a broken heart?

Collecting Words

I collect words.

Some come from Mr. Cooke's lessons,
big words about the big world:
        A-mer-i-ca
        Vir-gin-ia
I feel smart knowing the words,
even if I know nothing about anything
beyond Whitehaven's fences.

Some come from Master's newspapers.
Small words ripped out,
saved from being twisted and burned in his fireplace:
        Slave
        Sale
        Cook

Some I just sound out in my head myself.
        Fee-bee
        Mom-ma

But they's all mine.

I keep them hidden in the pages of Miss Tessa's old speller.
Bury it deep inside the hollow trunk
standing a mile or two inside the woods.

'Cause a slave can't have words.
Or hope.

But I do.
I got both,
buried deep in the hollow part of me.

Stranger

Any time Miss Tessa don't need me,
and Bea don't notice,
I sneak out to the woods,
to my sit-spot under the dead cottonwood tree,
long moss swaying lazy in its limbs.
Sometimes I hide more words
if I find some.
But most times,
I just sit and listen to the birds talk.

Teeka teeka
C*hit chit.*

I could even find their nests, had I a mind to.
They trust me.
I ain't no stranger.

But I don't trust strangers.

'Cause any time a stranger come,

I know something bad's about to follow.

Even birds know that.

The Hunt

Johnny Cooke would do anything I ask.
But he can't help it, he's smitten with me.
He's a hopeless teacher
but I did learn one thing from him:

my power.

I've toyed with his heart
and grown tired. Bored.
It was too easily captured
because Johnny Cooke is a boy.
I see that,
now that a man is here.

He arrived from the north today,
Doctor Ross Bergman:
          long of limb,
          broad shouldered,
          wealthy, well travelled, and well read.
          Dark curls. Thick beard. Deep eyes

I long to lure and hold.

Scholar.
Doctor.
Gentleman.

Mine.

Oh, yes.
I'm done with Johnny.
Besides, the hunt is far more exciting.

A P h o e b e S i g h t i n g

Miss Tessa sip her lemonade, eyeballing the dinner guest
while he talk to Master and Missus.
I can tell she like the look of him.
He young. He handsome, I suppose,
sitting there in his red vest,
his dark hair slicked back,
looking like a spring robin.

One that gots no idea the cat be on the prowl.

"But, Dr. Bergman," Miss Tessa say,
as I tip the water jug over his cup,
"it seems a long journey just to see some silly old birds."

That Doctor Birdman, open his sketchbook
right on the table.
He say some big words like
ornery-thollow-gee.
But I don't hear nothing when I see his drawings.
Birds pecking. Birds preening. Birds nesting.

Every one so real, they'd fly right off the sheet.

I don't know what kind of doctor he be,
but he surely is a watcher.
If he can draw like that, he see,
really see them,
like I do.

"Phoebe!" Missus snap.
And I realize the cup is full,
water spilling out my jug all over the table.

Before it spoil the book,
before it spill in Doctor Birdman's lap,
I grab the napkins and mop it up.
"Thank you," he smile, "Phoebe."
I swear, I near about dropped that jug right there.
Master have a lot of visitors
and I serve every one.
I flit in and out with food and drinks,
or flap that big feather fan,
or perch in my corner until they need me.
I's always invisible.

But that Doctor Birdman, he see me.
He looking right at me.
Right in me.
And I just want to disappear.

"She'd apologize," Miss Tessa say,
"but Phoebe can't talk. Still, she does a good chignon,
wouldn't you say?"
She pat her hair. Wait.
"It's lovely," Doctor Birdman say, and she blush,
like she done it herself.
"My Phoebe also has a way with birds. Healed its wing,"
Miss Tessa brag,
pointing at Yellowbird's cage in the corner.
"Too bad it's as mute as she is," Miss Tessa add,
like it my fault the bird don't sing.
Everybody laugh.

But me and Yellowbird,
we just watch.

Hatching a Plan

"A bird lover," Doctor Birdman say,
"Excellent! Ever see a Cedar Waxwing?"
They all looking at me now.
Miss Tessa. Master. The Missus.
I don't know what he talking about—
my eyes look at the door.
Surely Bea need me in the kitchen right this minute.

"Answer him, girl," the Missus say, her eyes cold.
"Yes or no."
I shrug.

Birdman smile at me. "It sounds like this." He whistle.
Bzee-bzee!

Oh, I know them. I nod.
I know where they is.

"Wonderful!" Birdman say.
"I'd love to see them while I'm here."

"Phoebe will take you," Master say. "Won't you, girl?"

Missus smile. But it don't reach her eyes,
it wallow on the bottom of her face like water in a rowboat.

Master tell Doctor Birdman
       that I'll be his guide,
       that I know'd the woods,
       that I know all about Virginian birding,
       and that the doctor won't leave Whitehaven
       unsatisfied.

Doctor Birdman keep his eyes on me,
his smile stretching wide his black beard.
My nerves start pecking like a chick in the egg.

Blowing Smoke

"What made you choose Whitehaven for your research?"
Tessa asks.

"Well, of course he'd stop here," I say.
"Any researcher worth his snuff
knows that Whitehaven is the cream of the Virginian crop."

I nod at Phoebe who fetches the humidor, as always,
to offer me a cigar from the cherrywood box.
Then Bergman.

"I don't smoke," he apologizes.

"Of course you do," I cut and light mine.
Hand it to him.
"You've just never tried the best. Right from my fields."

He hesitates and takes it. Drags. Coughs.

He wasn't lying. He doesn't smoke.

Hell, he grips it like a pencil.
"Like this." I take another. "You're going to draw *from* it—
not *with* it."

The ashy tip reddens as I suck and savor,
a smoky halo ringing my head.
"Whitehaven tobacco—the richest.
Be sure to put that in your book."

"But it's about birds, Father," Tessa says.

"Of *Virginia*," I add. "Besides,
it's high time you northerners
got a proper taste of the south."

I smile, take the small vial of tiny brown seed
from my pocket,
raise it, finger on the corked end, thumb on the other.
"My great-great-granddaddy built all this
from tiny seeds like these."

Bergman nods, draws on the brown tip.

"Five generations of seeding, pruning, harvesting, curing—
hundreds upon hundreds of slaves
working dusk to dawn
to make you that there cigar.
Now that's something, ain't it?"

But all Bergman does
is cough.

Five Generations

To grow strong leaves, prune the flowers and small buds.
To dry strong tobacco, cure it in the barn for a few weeks.
To manage strong slaves, bridle them with fear early on.

My daddy passed on everything he knew
about running a plantation
and on his deathbed, he gave me one last thing:
a vial of seed.
Every Master Duncan carried one tucked in his pocket
just like his daddy,
and his before that,
all the way back to Great-great-granddaddy,
the first Duncan, fresh from Scotland,
the one who built all this from nothing
but a handful of hardy seed
and a will of iron grit.
A reminder, my daddy said, closing my hand around a vial
of the Duncan fortitude,
the Duncan fortune,
and the duty of the Duncan who bears it

for the next generation.
Soil, seed, slave—nothing changes, son.

But he's wrong.

The times are changing.
>   North turns on South.
>   Slave against Master.
>   There's talk of war.

I am the first Duncan in five generations
who has no son.
>   But I blame Maggie.
>   After all, it was her jealousy
>   that shut me out when she was fertile.

I am the first Duncan in five generations
whose land is spent.
>   But I blame Brutus.
>   After all, it was his suggestion
>   that we seed fields that should lay fallow.

I need more money for more land—
and Bergman is the key.
>   He has to be.

Else I will be the first Duncan in five generations
to be the last.

Sweet and Sour

"Shad know them woods better than anyone,"
I say that morning.
"He should be the guide."
Phoebe shrug and pack the sandwiches.
We both know that fool couldn't track a chicken in a coop.
She reaches and takes down a bottle from the top shelf.

I notice, then, how tall she's getting,
like a slender sapling,
how even with that scar running cheek to jawbone
she's a beauty.

Missus still thinks
beauty come from ruffles and ringlets,
or the whiteness of your skin.
Years ago, she tried to spoil Phoebe
by cutting the outside,
but it don't change
what's inside.

What is.

Missus wanted to send Phoebe to work the fields
after Ruthie gone.
But I make Master Duncan his favorite, sugar pie,
and I ask him:

Master, I say.
Phoebe is no field slave.
That life would surely kill her.
Give her to me. I take care of her, like she's my own.
I teach her how to make your sugar pie
for when Old Bea can't no more.

And when Missus stomp her foot
and throw a hissy at the table that night,
I smile in the kitchen.
'Cause I know my Master.

When she serving bitter, sour words,
he choose sugar, any day.

My Phoebe

"And who gonna do your chores now?" I grumble.
"Me?"
I's angry, all right,
but not about the work.

I rest my hand on Phoebe's arm. "You heed old Bea,
stay with Miss Tessa."
Phoebe nod. Her honey eyes full of serious.

I shake my head. "Ain't nothing good come of being alone
with a white man."

I know she don't want to go. She scared.
But that's a good thing.
       Scared make us look.
       Scared make us listen.
       Scared make us run.
It's the nature-knowing that saves us.
You gotta listen to scared.
"Come here now, chicken." I gather her in,

wrap my thick arms around,
nestle her safe under my wing.
wishing I could keep her there.

When Missus cut my Phoebe's face with the knife,
I stitch her up.
And when Missus cut my Phoebe's back with the strap,
I cool her welts.
And when Missus cut my Phoebe down
with all the hate in her bitter soul,
I raise her up.
Time and time again,
I raise that girl
with all the love I got left in me to give.

"Beatrice!" Missus call from the front room.
I stiffen and let go.

"Get gone now. Silly child."
I hand Phoebe the heavy basket
and shove her to the back door.
"Poor you, gotta go walk in the sunshine
and listen to the birds,
while Old Bea working over a hot stove ..."

And step by step,
she walk away from me.

This must be how mother birds feel

when they shove their babies out of the nest
into a world of dangers.

R e s c u e

Shad always talk to me like we conversating.
Like he know what I might say.
Most times, he right.

"Don't go too far, now," he tease,
as I walk out the back yard with my basket.
"I don't want to have to come rescue you."

I look at him.
If anybody need rescuing, it's Shad.
Didn't Will pull his fool self outta the swamp
        when he near drown in it?
Didn't Will kill the snake that had him and Charlie
cornered in the barn, squealing like two piglets?
Didn't Will carry him home
        when he turned his ankle on his so-called hunt?
I look at his ankle, still sore from two weeks back.
Shad wag his finger at me.
"I know what you thinking—
but I caught you pheasant, didn't I?

And I know how my Phoebe like pheasant."

Way I heard it,
Charlie dared Shad to climb higher,
and Shad slipped and fell out the tree
on top of that poor old bird.

I shake my head and smile.
If I's ever in need of rescuing,

Shad surely be the worst one to do it.

Burned

"That's an awfully big basket."
Shad peek under the checkered cloth.
"Why don't you let me lighten your load?"

I turn away and he reach for the basket,
arm stretching 'round my shoulder.
I kind of like it there.
"Come on now, Phoebe.
Those two can't possibly eat all this."
He snatch a hot scone,
and I laugh as he bobble it in his burning fingers.

"Phoebe!" Missus call from the front porch.
I near drop my basket
as she come around the corner.
Me and Shad in a heap of trouble
if Missus know we stole from her.

I look at Shad standing there,
hand empty,

cheek lumpy,
eyes swimming.

"Quit your dawdling, foolish girl," Missus scold.
"The doctor and Tessa are waiting."
When she goes inside,
Shad spit a hot mess into his hand,
wave the other at his scalded mouth.
I shake my head.
Like Bea say,
If you play with fire, you gonna get burned.
But Shad can't help himself.
I guess that's what makes him Shad.

I guess that's why I like him so.

Chit Chat

Doctor Birdman don't seem happy that Miss Tessa
come with us in the woods.
But I don't mind.
Her chitter-chatter keep Doctor Birdman away from me.

I's free to walk ahead and find the trail.
I know where them waxwings is, I think.
But it don't matter none.

'Cause all of Miss Tessa's chitter-chatter
gonna keep the birds away from us, too.

To See a Bird

When I was little,
Momma used to walk with me in the woods on our way to
the Big House.
To see a bird, she say, *you gotta be*
> *still as a dusk pond;*
> *quiet as a white moth;*
> *and as patient as a grub snug in a cocoon.*
Root yourself in the dirt, she say,
> and we wriggle our toes in the cool earth.
Breathe in the big sky, she say,
> and I draw all the wide blue I could
> into my tiny chest.
Hold it deep inside your heart, she say, smiling.
And wait.

We'd stand there in the dawn light,
Momma and me, fingers to our lips,
listening to the leaves shush my heartbeat
until all was still.
Then come the morning song

of that bright red bird,
perched high in the branches above.

Birdie-birdie-birdie

Momma was right.
'Cause you gotta think you's part of the woods,
if you want that bird to believe it, too.

Deep in the Woods

"Are we there yet?"
We've been walking for ages,
and still no sign.
Of birds.
Of rest.
Of interest in me.

Be charming, Mother said.
Listen to his stories, she said.
Laugh at his jokes.
But the man never speaks.
Am I to feign interest in silence,
while we slog through the underbrush?

"Oh, the heat!" I say to his back.
But he presses on.
Surely this godforsaken wood has one bird in it.
Any bird will do.

"Are you sure you know where you're going, Phoebe?"

She nods and forges ahead,
leading us in circles,
leading us on.
She best find something soon,
fool of a girl,
or I'll strap her myself.

Hot on the Trail

I'm melting under all these damned petticoats.
A lady never swears.

A lady doesn't perspire.
But I am.
I feel it—my composure. Drip. Drip. Dripping away.

"Can we stop?" It's not a question.
"Phoebe, drink." I shouldn't have to ask.

She puts down the picnic basket.
Yet even under its load,
she's barely broken a sweat,
barefoot, brown, and breezy
in her cotton dress and blue headscarf.

But then, they're made for this weather, aren't they?

I sit in the shade,
flutter my fan,

bat my eyes.
But he is too busy looking at the treetops
for his waxtail whatever.

He knows all about bird behaviors,
and nothing of women.
Honestly, it's like I'm not even here.

Phoebe brings him another old nest.
"Look, Miss Tessa," he says,
like she's given him a handful of money, not muck.
"We're on the trail." He smiles. "He's elusive,
but we'll track him."

"Absolutely." I smile back.

Like I'm speaking of birds and not
a husband.

Squawking

Birds be every place in the woods, really.
Well, every place but here.
They long gone
or hiding, anyhow.

They hear Miss Tessa's cawing from a mile away.
"It's so hot."
"Are we there yet?"
"Can we rest now?"

Doctor Birdman know it, too.
He never gonna see no waxwing,
with all her chirp-chirping.

"What y'all find so exciting about birdwatching," she say,
"is beyond me."

Yes, I think to myself. *Yes, it is.*

"Let's have lunch," Doctor Birdman finally say.

'Cause there ain't nothing else to do.
I throw the blanket, set out all Bea's fixings:
      cheese and ham sandwiches,
      apple slices, sweet lemonade,
      and scones with strawberry jam.
Good thing Bea knows Miss Tessa's favorites.

'Cause when Miss Tessa eating,
our ears finally get a rest from all that squawking.

Birds Watching

We spend all afternoon wandering the woods.
When Miss Tessa grow tired of complaining,
a couple chickadees perch on high branches,
watching us with their pinhead eyes.
Heads tilting this way and that.

Who's watching who, Momma used to say.

Chick-a-dee-dee-dee-dee!
one warns,
then they fly away
before Doctor Birdman can open his sketchbook.

Momma told me the more *dee*s, the greater the warning.
People ain't always what they seem.
But nature don't lie, she say.

So I always listen to the birds.

And they say Doctor Birdman and Miss Tessa

be a four-*dee* danger,
each one surely on the hunt for something.

Rained Out

Fat rain tap the leaves.
I fetch Miss Tessa's parasol and hold it over her
while she fuss and fumble,
trying to keep her skirts and locks dry.

"Don't worry, Miss Tessa," Birdman tease,
"it's only a few raindrops."

"Oh, I know," Miss Tessa say,
"but I'm just so sweet,
I might melt like sugar in the wet."
I wonder if she know the same thing goes
for plain old salt.

I lift my face to the cool drops.
Let some tickle on my tongue.
But Miss Tessa move to leave,
so I follow,
careful to keep her parasol just so.
"Don't you think we should get back?"

she ask Birdman.
Even I know it ain't a question.
That doctor, though, he just stand there
looking at me,
at the treetops,
and finally at Miss Tessa, like he thinking of an answer.
I can tell he disappointed.

Everybody know, the best birdwatching be
right after a summer rain,
when the air cool
and the ground wet and wriggling with life.
That be when all them hide-a-birds come out,
looking for a bite and a bath.

And he gonna miss it.

Feeding Time

Bea eyeball me when I come in,
then nod at the pot cooling on the kitchen counter.
Sometimes it mush and beans,
but today it full of cornbread scraps and pot likker,
water from tonight's boiled greens.
"They been waiting on you."
I carry it out the back door, down the stoop,
around the corner
to where I know they's hiding,
watching me tip the trough and spill the muddy rainwater,
waiting for me to fill it from my pot.
They come a-running then,
elbowing for a good spot along the wooden sides.

Doctor Birdman watch from the stoop.
"Are those ... children?" he ask,
like he never seen one before.
I look at them:
        sack dresses dirty and wet,
        bare feet muddy

from walking up from the Quarters.
All knobs and knees, all rag and bone.
I nod.
Of course they's children. What he think they is?

"But," he say, "they're only babies."

True, some be only one or two summers old, if that.
But some's seen four or five.
They's just scrawny.
Master going set them to work soon.
Any one not fit for work—
he sell.

And nobody ever want to be sold.
Like Bea say: Better the devil you know
than the devil you don't.

They scoop sloppy handfuls to their mouths.
Soon enough, the trough empty.
The littlest one, Noah,
he run his fingers inside my bucket and lick them clean.
Doctor Birdman walk down off the porch.
Rain spots his shirt,
makes his slicked hair and moustache curls
droop and drip.
But he just stands there
like he don't even know it's raining.

He strange, that Birdman.
And I wonder what kind of devil he be.

Noah

The children shy away from
the white man standing in the rain.
Alls except Noah.
He ain't learned yet.
"Where's his mother?" Doctor Birdman ask,
kneeling in the mud,
meeting Noah face to face.
I point at the fields over yonder.
Noah lucky. He gonna see his momma at sunset.
But most of them won't. Most their mommas
got sold away.

Like mine.

Doctor Birdman look all confused.
Sad, even.
Don't he know the way of things?

Noah touch one of Doctor Birdman's dripping curls.
I s'pose he ain't never seen hair like that before up close.

His eyes go all big
and he smile.
Doctor Birdman take a biscuit out his pocket.
"A snack," he whisper, handing it to him, "to tide you over
until dinner."

It's a good thing I don't talk.
Else I gotta tell Doctor Birdman
this be the only meal they's getting today.

A New Word

"It's those damned abolitionists, I tell you!" Master say.
He slam his hand on the table at dinner,
making the women jump.
I don't know that word: *a-bo-li-tion-ist*.
But whatever it is, it sure got Master riled.
Even Shad look worried as he come in
with more wood for the fireplace.
"Why, just today," Master say,
"I read about a $1000 reward for the one
skulking around Norfolk a few weeks back.
Thirteen slaves went missing shortly after he did."

"That's terrible," Doctor Birdman pause,
a forkful of pie midair.
"Do they have a description?"
Master shake his head.
"Did they catch the slaves?"

"Two," Master say.
"Not much left of them

after the paddyroller's hounds got at them."

Shad look at me. I know he thinking about Will.
About what could have happened.

Doctor Birdman put down his fork,
like he ain't hungry no more.
"Such a waste."

"You're right. Theft, plain and simple," Master say,
as I clear away the plates.
"But I'll tell you this:
anyone trying to steal my slaves is going to wind up dead.
I have the right," he look at me and Shad,
"to protect my property."

And Shad and me smile and nod at our Master,
grateful.

On The Prowl

Mother enters my room the next morning,
carrying one of her ridiculous wide-brimmed hats.
"That sun is ruining your complexion."
Ever the critic, my mother.
She's right, though.
Damn her.

I glance in the mirror at Phoebe behind me,
dutifully pinning my hair,
as perfectly as she does every morning.
The sun has ruddied my cheeks and arms,
splattered my nose with freckles the color of dirt.
"A couple more days out there," I say,
"and I'll look like Phoebe's sister."

I feel Mother bristle, like Rufus,
hackles raised,
eyes narrowed.
I half expect her claws to come out.
She strikes lightning fast, slapping Phoebe's face,

scattering a handful of hairpins across the floor.

But Phoebe doesn't flinch, cower, or cry out.
She knows better.
She's learned it over the years.

"Leave us!" Mother shoves her aside.

And Phoebe slips away,
silent, as always.
In all the times she's been reprimanded,
I've never heard her make a sound.
Too bad she's gone mute.
Sometimes a whimper or two
is the satisfaction Mother's temper needs.

My Phoebe

We grew up together,
> Phoebe and I.
Two peanuts in a shell.
In truth, she was my only playmate.
We laughed and told stories,
we shared secrets,
we slept in the same room:
> my bed, a four poster
> and hers, a pallet of straw at the foot of it.
But we never noticed the difference
> of our beds;
> of our dresses;
> of our skin.
We hid from the dragon,
the fire and fang we knew as
Mother's wrath.
Those were long days of fantasy,
> when brave knights rescued us from castle towers,
> when dust held fairy magic,
> when a black girl and a white girl could be friends.

Such childishness.

It wasn't until my seventh birthday that I realized she was
        a slave.
Because that was the day she became
        my slave.
A gift given to me by my father
along with Sugar and Rufus.
        A pony.
        A kitten.
        A slave.
Just one more pet to own.

I think Phoebe stopped talking then.
I don't really recall.
I needed a servant—not a storyteller.
I wanted someone to pin my hair and press my clothes.
I no longer cared what she had to say,
        so long as she remained my faithful shadow.
And she has. Once I trained her.
I taught her so well,
my Phoebe often knows what I want or need
even before I ask.

Perhaps that is what angers Mother so much.
That Father gave Phoebe to me.

And not to her.

Drawing Lesson

Miss Tessa come birding with us again
and, surprise, surprise, we ain't seen no birds.
She blame me. Say I'm not tracking right.

So I take them to the honeysuckle bushes,
part the leaves and, sure enough,
huddled in the crook of the branch
in the bowl of a nest
bobble three tiny heads all peep-peeping
hungry for their momma.

"Yellow Warblers," he whisper, and sketch them on his pad
while I hold the branches open.
Warbler. That a new word for me.
But already, I think I knows how it look.
I tuck it inside my mind for later,
alone at my hollow tree.

"Funny," he say. "The mother usually swoops and shrieks
when the nest is threatened."

He right. It strange there's no sign of her.

"They make an awful racket," Miss Tessa say.
"She's probably away enjoying the silence."

Which make me think of Yellowbird.
What if these her chicks?
How long can they live without their momma?

What Is

My foot touch something and I look down
at the body of a baby bird,
broken from its fall.
Its bobble head, bald, blue veined,
and buckled in on one side,
its pink skin, ash gray.
It make me wanna cry.
But that strange Birdman,
he squat down
and draw that dead bird, too.

Why he wanna see that ugly sorrow?
Why he wanna know about
what can't be changed, fixed,
or undone?

Alls I know is some things
is what they is.

Some things best forgotten.

Weeding Out

After he draw the nest,
Birdman sit down and sketch weed after weed,
like he crazy.
Or aiming to drive Miss Tessa there.
She huff and puff,
cross her arms and tap her foot.

But it don't rush Birdman none.
He just smile.
Draw another sprig or stem.
Taking his sweet old time.

"Wonderful," Birdman say. "I can't find this species
in Canada."
And I get a tingle.

He's from Canada?
Canada is *real*?

Canada

Will say:
It's far.
And cold.
But slavery don't exist there.

Shad say:
You got cotton for brains, Will.
None of that is true.
If there are no slaves,
who takes care of the
masters and missuses?
And if there are no masters,
who takes care of
the Negroes?
He got a point.
Shad say:
Master build our homes,
and give us food.
And he do.
Shad say:

We wouldn't survive
without Master Duncan.
I s'pose we'd be like this here bird
thrown from its nest.
Shad say:
You older, Will,
but you ain't smarter,
not if you think things be better
in some cold,
far away place, up north
where you got
no one to care for you.
Your Canada don't exist.
it just some dream,
a wish for the weary,
a story for slaves scarred by
lashing or losing.
Believing in something
don't make it real.

Will shrug and say:
If you can't believe in it,
you never gonna see it.
But Shad, being blind to what is,
don't make it false.

All their words confuse me.
I don't know which ones is right.

A flock of geese
pass overhead,
a honking v
flying straight and true.
Geese.
Canada geese, I think as I watch them
move on,
and smile.

One Day

I never told Shad,
>   but I dreamed it, too,
>   after Momma left.
>   On those dark nights
>   when I reached for her
>   and felt as cold and empty
>   as the straw beside me,

>   I believed in Will's Canada.

>   *Maybe she there*, I say to myself.
>   *And maybe,*
>   *one day,*
>   *she come back and take me there, too.*

Nest

I climb way up the white trunk of the tremble-tree,
and get Birdman another nest I seen
amongst the flutter-leaves,
a tiny cup of twig and straw.
A home once.
It empty now, but he thank me and draw it just the same.

Then that Doctor Birdman
he stick it in his pocket and climb that tree himself.
He inch along that thick branch,
getting his pants all wrinkles and dirt.
He reach in his pocket, stretch out along the limb,
and settle that bird nest right back where I found it.

"Why bother?" Miss Tessa call up.
"It's just a mess of mud and sticks."

Doctor Birdman jump down and brush his hands.

"It's a home, Miss Tessa," he say.

"And as any good birder knows,"
he smile at me for a second,
"You just never know
when the mother might return."

Something

Birdman a watcher,
like Momma was—
seeing the world eyes wide open
when most white folk too busy seeing theyselves.

He know about birds,
like Momma did—
listening to the wisdom of wing and feather
when most people stay deaf to the song.

But he still a white man.
Like Bea said.

And like most, he after something.
I can tell by the way he look at me,
I got something he want.

Only I don't know what that something is.

Make Him

Enough of this nest nonsense
and wandering through woods.
"We'll lunch by the fields, Phoebe," I announce.

Linking my arm in his,
I pace him to my stride—
make him linger,
make him listen,
make him long for me.
Mother was right.
Any man can be led like a workhorse,
if you take the reins.

Of course, as soon as we leave the woods,
birds sing.
Doctor Bergman whistles back, note for note.
"Spot on," I say, as though it were a useful skill.
It makes him smile.
And that makes me blush—
a glow that draws men as surely as moths.

"But the mockingbird's got me beat," he says.
"It can mimic over a hundred songs."

If he's impressed by that, wait until I tell him
we have almost a hundred slaves.

Songs of Wood And Field

I lead him to the knoll,
eager to show him the richness and beauty
that is my home,
that is me, really.
One day, this will all be mine:
rolling fields,
long, lush rows of tobacco plants
where a hundred slaves
cut and tie,
and cut and tie,
leaving bundle after bundle in their wake.

"Here." I stick my parasol in the grass, staking my claim,
signaling to Phoebe to set out our luncheon.

Hoe, Emma, hoe.
A song, rich and slow, carries on the warm breeze,
from the fields below.
Hoe, Emma, hoe.
You turn around, dig a hole in the ground.

Hoe, Emma, hoe.

"Now there's a song I bet you don't know," I tease, and this time, it's me that mimics:

Lord send my people into Egypt Land.
Hoe Emma hoe.
Lord strike down Pharaoh and set them free.
Hoe Emma hoe.

Mimicking

One young picker fall behind
as the line move from stalk to stalk.
It Ella Mae.
Brutus loom over her, crack his whip,
make the song skip a beat,
when she fall,
but the workers move on without her,
else they next.

Hoe, Emma, hoe.

A small boy run the line with his water bucket.
With his bad leg, he must be Nate.
Poor Nate, only a few weeks gone
since I seen him at the trough.
Still, I's glad to see him kneeling by Ella Mae,
giving her water.
She hateful mean, she is.
But even Ella Mae don't deserve what Brutus give.

Miss Tessa explain how slaves work
from sun up to sun down:
planting, pruning, or plucking hornworms.
Leaves all thick and green, now,
time to cut, bundle,
and thread them on sticks
for hanging in the curing barn up the hill.
She talk like she done it all herself.
"Brutus does a good job keeping them in line,"
Miss Tessa say,
mimicking her daddy now.
"They're known to be lazy, like that girl.
Others just can't be trained."

Birdman don't say nothing.
Just stare at the field where Ella Mae
drag herself up and back in line.

"We buy, breed, feed, clothe, house, and train them,"
Miss Tessa parrot.
"And if need be, we sell them.
But we take good care of our property."

"Your *people*," he say.

"Oh, Doctor," she roll her eyes,
and say what master always say,
"they're not people ...

they're Negroes."

Hand - Me - Down

Phoebe silently
sets out sandwiches, lemonade, and sugar pie,
flicking crumbs off our tartan blanket
with her soft, brown hands.
"That will do," I say,
dismissing her to sit nearby
in my hand-me-down dress
to eat the broken pie crust
and a small cup of lemonade;
a treat I said she could have.

Where would the poor girl be
without me?

Without me,
she'd be on the line,
hacking leaves under the noonday sun,
instead of watching from the shade.
Without me,
she'd be sleeping in some crowded cabin in the Quarters,

instead of having a pallet all to herself,
in the hall outside my room.

Without me,
that girl would have no purpose. Plain and simple.
No training. No nothing.

I'll admit, Phoebe works hard—
but the work isn't hard at all.
How hard could it be
to take care of little old me?
With all I hand-her-down,

Phoebe's got it easy.

Divine Right

"Slaves are born to serve us,"
I explain to Doctor Bergman.
It says so right in the Bible.
Verses preached from pulpits
since before I can remember.
"Why ... it's our divine right."

"Teach slaves
to be subject to their masters
in everything,
to try to please them,
not to talk back to them.
That's from Titus," I say,
"but I know them all."

He smiles. I love his smile. "Things are different up north."

"But the Bible," I say,
"surely that would be the same everywhere."

"Yes," he says, "but some people
... misinterpret
even God's truth."

Fools, maybe.
The good Lord put it right there in black and white.
Who am I to argue that?

"Well, here at Whitehaven, we do right by our slaves."
I look with pride across the lush field.
Let the song fill my head.

"And they're happy." I sip my lemonade.
"Just listen to them singing."

Secret Songs

Will told me about that song one time.
He learned it from his daddy who worked the fields.
It code.
One of the secret songs that
say one thing and mean another.
Most field songs is.

Sure they keep pick and hoes in time, or spirits up,
like music do.

But I know something Miss Tessa don't.
Something Brutus don't.
Something even Master don't know.

It ain't about slaves in Egypt.
And the Pharaoh they strike down
ain't no Egyptian neither.

Miss Tessa know the words
but she don't know the truth.

'Cause if she did,
she might not wanna eat her sugar pie
and join the chorus of
a hundred sweaty workers
singing secret songs
about killing her daddy.

Divining Wrong

Miss Tessa know the words,
from the Bible,
from the song,
from her daddy and his daddy before him.

But she wrong—
they ain't singing 'cause they happy.
And they ain't singing 'bout Moses neither.

Makes me wonder if there be other
truths
she got wrong.

What I Desire

Fair hair and skin.
Bright blue eyes.
Slender of arm and waist.
With a flirtatious smile ever on her lips
and a fortuitous inheritance on her horizon,
Miss Tessa truly is every southern gentleman's dream.

But I'm no southern gentleman.

I will endure her incessant chatter
as she brags and preens
and struts about,
flapping fans
and fluttering eyes,
so eager to show me her
southern hospitality.

She's not built for birding.
Or heat.
Or walking.

Or waiting
while I draw weed after weed.

She'll give in, soon enough,
and then I'll finally have
what I truly desire:

time alone with Phoebe.

Black-Eyed Susan

Miss Tessa in a snit.
Missus told her she can't go in the woods tomorrow
with Doctor Birdman.
It Tuesday.
Missus say she gotta do her lessons with Mr. Cooke.
"You treat me like a child, mother!" She stomp her foot.

But there's two of them in it.
Missus do treat Miss Tessa
like she still a young girl in braids.
But most times,
Miss Tessa act like one.

I set the vase of flowers on the dining room table
like Missus ask,
while Bea pour the tea,
like Missus ask.

"*Arethusa bulbosa*," she say to her daughter,
as she cup her hand around a purple blossom.

"You know, this orchid only blooms for a month,"
I don't has to look at Miss Tessa to know she sulking.
"It's valuable. Highly sought, because it's rare," Missus say.
"Not some Black-eyed Susan."
She take Miss Tessa's hands.
"You need to decide what you are, sweetie.
No man is going to believe you are a delicate orchid,
something rare and sweet and precious,
if you are acting like some common weed."

Miss Tessa clench her jaw.
But even I know, she gonna heed Missus,
like she always does.

I follow Bea back in the kitchen
where she start buzzing as she baking.
"*Arethusa bulbosa,*" she snort. "I ain't *never* heard of that.
It's *called* Dragon-mouth 'cause it look like a dragon,"
she mutter,
"and it come from the swamp."
She slam the pastry dough on the counter
and pound it with her fist.
"Hmph! Give me a Black-eyed Susan, any day."

Without Miss Tessa

The woods going to be awful quiet tomorrow,
without Miss Tessa.

Doctor Birdman
can draw all the weeds he like
and all the nests he like
for as long as he like
without Miss Tessa.

He might even see that Cedar Waxwing
without Miss Tessa
talking and squawking,
scaring all the birds away.

Still,
I's awful nervous to be going in the woods,
with Doctor Birdman,

without Miss Tessa.

Alone With Doctor Birdman

I do like Bea say:
I lead Doctor Birdman where he wanna go,
deep in the thick of the wood.
But I keep my distance.
And while he keeping an eye on the treetops,
I be keeping an eye on him.

We stop for lunch and I set up his picnic, like always.
Roast chicken leg, potato salad, and Bea's lemonade.
And when he sit down to eat,
I perch on a fallen log
out of reach,
where I can see him,
and pick at my cornbread.

Momma's Birds

Doctor Birdman lie on the blanket in the shade,
say he gonna take a nap.
It sure is something hot,
even the birds quiet now,
sheltered in the shadows,
saving their songs to sing the sun down.

He must like the quiet here, just like me.
'Cause he sure ain't getting none back at the Big House.
Not with all the Duncans chirping at him
all his waking hours.

I wait until he snoring
and then I sneak away
to where I can't hear him snore no more,
to where I hear them,

Momma's birds,

calling my name.

Peanuts

I sneak my jar of peanuts outta the hidey-hole and sit
under the hollow tree,
breathing slow,
listening to the cicadas creak and buzz in the hot air.

The jar almost full.
I been collecting peanuts ever since
Momma showed me years ago
where to find them.
Master love his peanuts, she say.
But sometime he so eager to get cracking on the next shell
he forget each one got two *nuts inside.*

Seem crazy to me to throw away what you want
when it's sitting right there in your hand.

That first night, after he done,
Momma and me sweep up the mess
he left all around his leather chair.
And back in our small cabin

we sit on our dirt floor and sort through the heap
of torn tan husks and dark skins Master toss away,
'til we find all them half shells that ain't been cracked.
Each like a tiny egg.
And when I split one open, sure enough,
inside be a perfect peanut.

You see, Phoebe? Momma say.
Just 'cause the Master don't want it,
don't mean it ain't good.
Everything the good Lord made
got a purpose.

A Song for Me

Momma and me, we filled half the jar that night.
I's so excited—I just wanted to eat them all.
But Momma say, *Wait.*

The next day, she take me by one hand
and the jar in the other
and lead me out here.
She put one nut in my small palm and hold it out.
Be still, she say.
I don't know what she at,
I just wanna eat that peanut.
Why she teasing me?

Then a small bird
hover over us,
flitting this way and that,
deciding if we belong.
I stays still as a stalk,
watch his wings flutter, watch him swoop down,
grip my pinkie like a perch in his little back claws.

Head tilting,
he watch me with that black bead eye,
ruffle his brown tail,
settle his wings.

Up close, I see he ain't just a bird,
he a million perfect little feathers,
a curious mind,
and a tiny soul pitter-patting in his cotton-boll chest.
He peck that peanut,
pinch it in his black nib beak
and, just like that,
he gone,
swooping back to the branch of the hollow tree.

Wide-eyed, I look at Momma.
We watch that little brown bird eat that peanut
and before he go, he sing for us.

Fee-bee! Fee-bee!

"He saying my name, Momma," I whisper,
sure my soul about to burst out my small chest.
"Did you hear?"

Momma smile at me,
tears in her eyes.
  And I know she heard it, too.

All these years I been sifting through Master's shells
and saving up the peanuts.
Sure the birds like them.
But the truth is,
I'd dig through a thousand shells for just one nut
to hear Momma's birds
sing my name.

Two Phoebes

Time is running out.
I must make my move.
Soon.

Now.

After all, Phoebe and I are finally alone.
Who knows when that might happen again?

I leave the picnic blanket and easily follow her trail:
bent twigs, footprints, crushed blades.
She's quiet,
but not invisible.

Will she do what I ask—
or will she run and tell her Master?
That is always the risk, I suppose.
Choosing a mute this time,
might work to my advantage.

Tracking her through the dense wood,
I come to a clearing.
In the center stands the trunk of a long dead tree
stripped of bark and branch,
smooth and hollowed with time.
At its base sits Phoebe:
      legs crossed,
      arm out like a slender branch,
      hand cupped like a small brown nest.

A tiny bird flits between the tree and her hand:
Eastern Phoebe.
Common, really.
And yet, in the dappled light of the lush wood,
I consider the bird,
the girl,
the moment.

Rare Phoebe sightings:
      the wary bird, so at ease around a human.
      the nervous girl, so at home in the wood.
The bird sings.
The girl smiles.
And I realize,
I have never seen anything
so beautiful.

Our Little Secret

Birdman awake when I get back.
He look at me strange.
Or maybe it just strange that he look at me.
I like it better when I's invisible.
Nothing good ever come outta being noticed.

"Phoebe." He step toward me.

     I step back.

"I'm glad we're out here alone." He smile.

     I don't.

"I was hoping you might do me a favor."
He don't take his eyes off me.

     My heart flapping in my chest—
     Get away! Get away!

"You can't tell anyone—" he say,
"not even Shad or Beatrice.
It has to be …

our little secret."

The Promise

"Can you do that, Phoebe,
can you keep a secret?"
He come closer.
Close enough to grab me.

But he don't.

"I trust you," he say, "because, well,
because the birds trust you."
He sit on the trunk beside me.
And I let go of the breath I's been holding.

"I need to talk to one of the slaves. But not just any slave.
He needs to be someone strong,
someone the others respect."
He watching me, close.
"Someone," he say, "who maybe tried to escape before?"

He tilt his head.
"Do you know someone like that, Phoebe?"

I nod.

"Wonderful." Birdman smile.
"Tonight I need you to bring him
to the hollow tree
where you feed the birds. Can you do that?"

He know about my tree?
What else he know?

"I promise to keep your secrets safe." He hold out his hand.
"Will you do the same for me?"

I swallow and nod.
Shake inside as I shake his hand.

But when a white man ask for something—
what else you gonna do?

D r a w n

Birdman open his pad to his last page.

My breath catch.

It's Momma,
sitting by the hollow tree,
smiling as one of her *fee-bee* birds
takes a peanut from her hand.

She beautiful.
Just like I remembered her.

I look at him like he some kind of voodoo—
       drawing birds so real, I swear I hear them sing,
       drawing memories outta my head and
       Momma right out of my heart.

I look back at the picture
drawn to her face, her smile, the scar tracing her cheek,
realizing

it ain't Momma—

it's me.

Storm Coming

I don't like that Bird Doctor.
No, sir.
I seen him watching Phoebe, when no one else is looking.
And just like how Bea know when a storm's coming,
I know
deep in my bones,

something just ain't right.

So when Bea say they's going in the woods alone,
I follows them.
I see him sneak and spy on Phoebe,
draw her, even, from where he hide in the bush.

Who do that, I ask you?

Now, maybe he is a bird doctor and maybe he ain't.
Alls I know for sure is that
it ain't the birds he after.

When he move in close to my Phoebe,
whisper secrets,
take her hand,
I's about ready to explode outta them bushes
like a crack o' lightning.

Only he let go
and show her his book.

Yes.
Storm's a-coming.

Only, just like Bea,
no one gonna believe me
until they caught up in it.
And by then,

it too late.

A Gift

I tuck Birdman's drawing inside my mind,
hide it deep.
He got a gift, that Birdman.
And he gave me one, too.
'Cause his drawing
remind me of who Momma was.
But more than that,

it remind me of who I is.

Broke

I've got hundreds of tobacco sticks loaded with leaves,
ready for curing,
just lying where they left them in the fields.

Damn those lazy Negroes.

Brutus needs to crack the whip,
lay down the law,
pick up the slack,
motivate them!

Clearly, they aren't working hard enough,
or fast enough.
And none of them is smart enough to see:
every leaf is like a dollar.
I won't stand by while my money
wilts and withers in the hot sun.

I need all the muscle I've got in the Quarter,
so I let Will out.

The stubborn mule,
he isn't broke yet,
but the way things are going,
if I don't get this harvest in,

I might be.

Hot Water

When I's done rolling rags in Miss Tessa's hair
and she done calling me for this or that,
I lie on my straw bed in the dark hall outside her door
as the Big House sigh and settle itself to sleep.
But I can't—
my mind bubbles and boils like soup.

Maybe it a trick.
Maybe Birdman just want to get me alone
in the woods at night.

But
            we already was alone;
            he coulda done what he liked had he a mind to.
            Besides, this time, I'd be bringing Will.
No, it ain't about me.
Birdman want words with a slave.

But
            how come he need to speak to someone like Will?

and what he got to say
that can't be said in day light?
and why he need me to bring him?

I can't do it.
I won't.
    Secret words ain't allowed.

But
    ain't I got my own?
    Birdman know about my tree—
    maybe he know about my secret words, too.
If I don't go,
    Birdman gonna tell Master I can read and write.
If I do go,
    Master gonna find out I's sneaking out at night.
Either way,
I be pickled, peeled, and locked away forever.
Or worse,
sold down south.

Alls I know is,
I's in hot water.

Whippoorwill

Come midnight,
the moon just a sliver in the sky,
I creep down to the Quarters,
past forty ramshackle huts and sheds
as tired and weary as the field folk inside.
The whole world sleeping,
'cept for me
and that whippoorwill calling in the dark.

I tiptoe to the last shack where
Will's snores rumbling out loud and clear.
Even when the door groan open,
them five or six men sleep on like the dead,
spent from a long day's labor.

In a few hours, Brutus be blowing that horn,
getting them up long before that rooster wake the sun.

Will so big,
even in the dim light of the cabin

I know which one is his
slumped shadow.
I tiptoe over, touch his arm, and he wake.

"Phoebe? What's wrong?"

I wave for him to follow me.
And he do,
yawning and scratching his back.
I s'pose his scars and scabs still trouble him some.

"What kinda trouble that Shad got he'self in now?"
Will grumbles,
as I lead him into the dark wood.
Only Shad ain't the one in danger this time.

Whip-poor-will! Whip-poor-will!

That nightbird know as plain as I do what gonna happen
to Will,
to both of us,
if Master find out.

Night Whispers

Will freeze beside me when he see
it ain't Shad
waiting in the clearing by the hollow tree.

It Birdman.

Will crouch, try to pull me down,
but I shake my head
and wade into the puddle of moonlight,
leaving Will where he hide.
Birdman nod at me, walk over to the bushes, and stop.
"Knowledge is the key to your cage,"
he whisper at the leaves.
"Get any men you trust
and meet here tomorrow at midnight."

Will don't move. Don't make a sound.
Even when Birdman turn
and disappear into the shadow of the woods.
I wonder if Will gone, too—

'til he burst through the bushes
and grab me,
fingers like iron shackles on my skinny arms.

"What you tell him?" he say, rattling me.
I never seen Will so angry.
I shake my head.
I never say nothing to nobody, he know that.

He frown. "Why he ask for me?"
I shrug. I ain't about to tell him
that it was me that chose Will.

"Don't you know how dangerous this is, Phoebe?
What Master would do?"
My eyes fill up.
I nod slowly.
I know.
Lord, I know what we risking just by being here.

He let go, rub his hands on his head,
look at the darkness around us,
then back at me.
"This never happened.
We never here.
I don't want nothing to do with that white man," he say
before he storm away.

Will is terrifying when he mad.

but I know he ain't angry with me,
not really.

Big Will scared.
For both of us.

And I swear, that is even more terrifying.

Pe a Po d s

I sit in the kitchen shelling pea pods,
thinking on what Birdman whisper to Will last night;
peeling back what he say
to get at what he really mean.
But alls I got is more questions:
>How can knowledge be a key?
>And to what cage—
>>Will already free from the curing barn,
>>and you don't even need a key for that.
>>Far as I know,
>>storehouse the only building that's locked,
>>so slaves don't steal the Master's food.
It strange.
Shad strange, too,
asking me if I's going with Birdman again today,
fussing over me every time he come in that back door.
I can't even make water without him a-calling for me.

Bea say the Doctor gone out birding by hisself this time.
Early this morning he go, with his backpack all loaded up.

"Is he gone for good?" Shad ask, excited-like.

"He better not be," she say.
"Else the Missus gonna be some sore
after she and Missy plan this here spread on his account."
She shake her head and shove the dozen hens in the oven.
"I swear, Master invite half of Virginia here tonight
to meet the Doctor.
What he trying to prove—
when the storehouse near empty?"

I stop shelling. Look at Bea.

"Don't mind that, now," she say, hands on her wide hips.
"Alls you need to worry about
is getting them peas in that bowl."

But Bea wrong.
I gots a lot more worries than that.

If You Ask Me

Missus carries the key to the storehouse.
She knows what we got
and what we don't.

If you ask me,
the way she's acting, you'd think things are
the same as always.
But they sure ain't.

She read me the menu,
tell Old Sam she want the red rose china set out,
the silver polished,
and the room scrubbed top to bottom.
Sam tell me Master invite some businessmen from town,
old men Master got nothing good to say about,
other than they's rich.

If you ask me,
sounds like Master setting them out around his table
just like the china we never use.

Meanwhile, Tessa be
calling Phoebe up there every ten minutes
to help her peel off that dress and stuff her in another
or whip up another hairstyle,
or garnish her with bits and bobs.

Hell, if anything need peeling—it the potatoes.
If anything need stuffing or garnishing—it the hens.
And if anyone need learning—
it those Duncan women.

I know what they up to.
Any fool can see they's trying to impress that doctor.
Had they asked me,
I would've set them straight,
saved a whole lot of trouble:

No man cares about
         whether your china got roses or not
         your dress got ruffles or not
         or your hair got ringlets or not.
The best way to impress a man,
any man,
is through his stomach.

Only nobody ask me.

Seat of Honor

Daddy invited men of means to dinner tonight.
Masters all.

"She's of age," Mother said to Daddy
when they thought I wasn't listening.
"Time to start thinking about a good match
for Whitehaven."

"Way ahead of you, dear," Daddy said.

He sits me next to Doctor Bergman
at the table of mother and men.

I laugh at the doctor's stories,
lean in
to touch the doctor's arm,
and ask
about his work,
just so he will look at me
and not them.

I suppose I can have the pick of any Master's son.
Lanky lads my age,
all elbows and Adam's apples.
Masters of nothing
but boyish longings
as they slurp their soup,
stealing red-faced looks at me,

wishing they were sitting in Doctor Bergman's seat.

Troubles

I's run ragged getting ready for the big dinner,
pulled between what Bea need and what Miss Tessa want.
Children waiting at the trough.
Master waiting at the table.
Everybody hungry.
I feel like a momma bird
flitting in and out and in and out that kitchen door
so many times my head spin.
Birdman kept so busy feeding their curiosity
he don't notice me.
And I's kept so busy feeding their bellies,
I ain't got time to notice if he did.
I's about ready to drop
when Master finally take them to the study—
for cigars and whiskey.

After they go, I load up on dirty dishes,
head back into the kitchen
relieved to know
that I made it through the day and dinner

without spilling nor breaking a thing,
that my long day is almost over,
that Bea gots two Quarter girls up to do the washing.
Then I see,
one of them's Ella Mae.

And I know my troubles only starting.

Hot and Bitter

"Poor Yellagirl look tired," Ella Mae tease,
when Bea leave the kitchen.
Ella Mae older than me by at least five summers,
but she always act like a child.

"Is work too hard for your soft, yellow hands?"
She snicker with her friend.

I don't know why she always call me yellow.
I's light brown—like coffee with cream.
She coffee too, only dark.
Hot and bitter.
Maybe it's the sun.
Maybe I'd be that way, too,
if I cut crops all day long.
Working fields make their skin darker,
their hands tougher, muscles stronger.
And for some reason,
it make Ella Mae hate me even more.
I never know why it matter so much,

what color on the outside
or what I ever done to Ella Mae.
She been mean to me since
Momma left.

"You think you better than us," she hiss,
"but you ain't.
Just 'cause you live here in the Big House,
just 'cause you Missy's plaything,
picnicking while we toil in the sun,
you still nothing."
She look me over, disgusted.
"Acting all white. Like you one of them.
You ain't one of them. And you ain't one of us.
You is *different*.
You a nobody, Yellagirl. And nobody want you."
She smile.
"Not even your momma. Why you think she leave you?"

I don't know why it hurt me so.
She say it all the time.
And each time like I hearing it fresh.
I don't hear nothing else:
not Bea scolding
not Shad calling
and not three red rose plates smashing on the floor
where I drop them
as I run out the back door.

My Phoebe

I find her at her sit-spot under the deadwood tree.
All tears and snuffles.
"Don't cry, Phoebe," I say. I can stand anything but that.
She wipe her face on her sleeve.
"I heard what Ella Mae said," I tell her.
"She wrong. You know that?"

Phoebe shrug.

"She wrong. About you, about your momma,
about all of it."

Phoebe nod slowly.

"Why you let that fool girl inside your head?" I ask.
"You smarter than that."
I pause,
reading her face,
knowing her fears.
"There's a part of you that wonders about your momma,

about why she left you."
I swallow. "I feels the same way about Will.
How could he leave without me?
Will and me was all each other got."

I wait until my voice don't wobble.

"Ella Mae right about one thing, though," I say.
"We ain't one of them—
not the whitefolk and not the field slaves.
But we still somebody, you and me.
Ain't Bea always saying that?
'*Boy*,' I stand, hand on my hip, just like her,
'*you sure is* something.'"

Phoebe smiles
and suddenly,
I feel like I could do anything.
Be anything.
Endure anything.
For her.

I hold out my hands and pull her to her feet,
but I don't let go.
"Ella Mae jealous. And she wrong ...
Somebody want you.
I do."
I lean in slow,
kiss her soft smile

and melt inside.

"You's my Phoebe," I whisper.

"I'll always watch out for you.

I promise you that."

On his Plate

I sweep the broken china in a pile
after I send them fool girls back to the Quarter.
That Ella Mae,
she lucky I didn't break the whole set over her head.

"Accident or not," Sam say,
as he put the good silver back in the box,
"Missus ought to know."

"And what then?" I stop and face him, hand on my hip.
"She'll make Phoebe pay for this.
Ain't the poor girl paid enough?"

"And what happens when Missus has another big dinner
and tells me to get out the good china, Bea?
What then?"

"If Missus ask why she short three plates,
I'll tell her," I say.
"But there ain't no use in upsetting her about it now.

You know as well as I do, Samuel,
Master got enough on his mind
without her jawing at him
over three silly old side plates."

Sam chew the inside of his cheek.
He know what I mean.

"She ain't gonna need them anytime soon."
I lower my voice. "I hear the field hands talking,
this crop's weak, the soil spent—
hell, I seen the empty shelves.
I don't need to see Master's ledger
to know he in trouble."
Sam say nothing about what he know.
The way he hang that old white head,
I know
what he know is worse than I thought.
Sam loyal to Master. And the Master before him.
He live all his long years doing what Master need.

"Master got enough on his plate," I say.
"The last thing he need
is old Missus nagging."

He nod.
I pat his hand,
thank him for saving Phoebe
for now.

But we don't smile.
'Cause we both know,
when Master in trouble,

we all is.

Answers

Long after Shad leave,
I sit in the dark by my tree,
thinking
about Ella Mae and Momma,
about Shad and me,
and, strangely enough—
about Birdman's key.

Seems my mind full of questions, but no answers.
How is knowledge a key?
Bea say, *If you wait, the answer done come to you.*

So I climb into my hollow tree.
Burrow down in its bottom.
And wait to know.

W h o

Through the knothole, I see
a shadow creeping closer to the clearing.

Who-WHO! Who-WHO!
owl asks.
In the slim moon's light, I see who—
Birdman.

He walk right up to the tree
like he knows I's inside.
Like he gonna reach in and grab me.
But he don't.
Instead, he turn and sit,
lean against the smooth trunk,
and wait.

I don't move.
Barely breathe
as we sit in silence
separated by a bit of wood.

according to Phoebe

Now that he's here,

I's terrified.

Who-WHO! Who-WHO!
owl warn.
Reminding me I know nothing about this man,
except that he is not
who he say.

156 | The Gospel Truth

Courage

"You came," his voice rumble,
and I near jump outta my skin.
I's just about to poke my head out the trunk and surrender
when I hear others whispering.

Will come rustling out the shadows
and walk toward Birdman.
I guess he curious, too.
Behind him come Levi, Joe, and Davey.
"This dangerous business, sir," Will say.

"Risky business for all of us." Birdman stand.

"This here's the men I trust."
Will speak it like Birdman ain't one.
Yet.

"You've shown great courage, coming here tonight,"
Birdman say.
"And you're going to need lots more of it,

if what I've brought interests you."

He reach into his bag and hold something
small and round
in the palm of his hand,
glinting like gold in the moon's light.
And I wonder
if that the key.

The Risk

Four strong males.
I had hope there might be more.
But I would do all this,
risk all this,

for even one.

What I Know

"I am a doctor, yes,
I study birds,
but that is not why I am here.
I've come to the South to give you
the key to freedom:
knowledge."

I pause.

"Many men, like Will, have tried to be free,
but don't know where or when to run."

Will nods.

"Others, so broken by the bonds and lash,
can't even dare to think such a thing is possible.
But I'm here to tell you
it is.
And I can show you how."

They exchange glances of disbelief.

"I can show you routes" I say,
"teach you friend from foe,
because you have friends
beyond the borders of Whitehaven.
Not every white man is like your master.
I may be the first you've met,
but believe me:
there are hundreds more like me,
and hundreds more,
like you,
who have escaped from slavery
to live up north,

free."

Words of A White Man

I hand them what I've brought.
Each man silent,
as he stands in the moonlight considering what he holds:

> a compass
> a knife
> a pistol
> twenty dollars

> a chance at freedom.

"I can give you the tools," I say,
"to guide and protect you.
I can show you the path,
but in the end,
it's you that must choose it
and walk it.
You alone that must risk it."

I watch them weigh it.
Each man wondering if he's willing

to wager his life
on the words of a white man
in the woods at midnight.

The Plan

"Think carefully on what I've said," Birdman say,
"and if you choose not to run,
I beg you
not to speak a word of what was said here tonight.
All of our lives
depend on it."

He hold out the bag and they put their gifts inside.

"Gather what provisions you can," Birdman say,
"take this sack and
meet at Carson's Corners
ten days from now.
Saturday night.
Hide in the ditch,
watch for my wagon.
Wait for the signal."

He stand with his back to me
and I don't see the signal.

coo-WOO   woo-woo-woo
a lone mourning dove calls,
sad and soulful in the dark of night.

Birdman bundle the sack,
turn around and drop it down the tree trunk.
It tumble on top of me,
blade cutting through burlap
and stabbing my arm,
deep.
I bite my lip,
so hard it bleed, too,

but I don't make no peep.

Stained

Long after the men leave,
I sit in that hollow tree listening to the night,
waiting to feel safe enough to climb out.
But I don't.
I doubt I'll ever feel safe again.
Even as I walk back to the Big House,
it feel like their secrets are all over me,
that anyone who sees me
will know I know.

Brutus already up
sounding his horn,
calling the workers to the field.
So I sneak 'round the far side to the well.
The knife cut is bleeding pretty bad,
dripping down my forearm and fingers.
It should sting something awful,
but my mind so numb from all I heard
I barely feel it.

Can Birdman be trusted? He white.
Why he wanna help slaves? He could get killed for that.

Unless the Master already know.

Maybe he and the Master just
testing big Will.
Seeing if he take the bait.
Will he?

Seems the more answers I get—the less I knows.

I stop at the well
and wash my forearm with a bucket of water.
Take off my blue head scarf and bind it tight.
It deep, that cut,
bleeding through blue.
Blood on my skirts, too.
Beet-red drops dripped down the front.
There, now, forever.

Everyone carry secrets inside,
but once they spilled
there ain't no taking them back.
And just like blood,
everyone that secret touches

be stained.

Connecting the Dots

Early morning
the best time for hunting dove.
I's out with my slingshot and sack,
sure I'll get four, maybe five.
But then I sees a drop of blood
still wet on a leaf
and another up ahead.
I follows them deep into the wood,
hoping they lead me to a wounded deer.
I can just see they faces when I come home with it
draped across my shoulders.
Oh, they gonna love Shad then!

I lose the trail a couple times,
worry this light rain
gonna wash it away
before I reach the end.
But I's a tracker. I is.
Nothing gets past Shad.

The last drop leads me to the clearing
away in the woods,
where I kissed my Phoebe.
I ring 'round the tree trunk
but there's no sign of deer, or rabbit,
not even one crippled dove.
I scratch my head,
walk in circles
as the rain start lashing.

Then slowly head for home
with nothing to show for my morning's hunt
but an empty wet sack.

Seeping Out

Phoebe come all frazzled and frizzy
through the back door,
looking like something Rufus drag in.

"Where's your kerchief?" I scold.
She never goes without her headscarf.
It ain't allowed.
Missus don't like seeing Phoebe's hair.
She hate them soft, loose curls.
Then I see it wrapped 'round her arm,
seeping red.
"Is that blood?"

I wring a rag, wipe her weary face
before I start on her forearm.
"Don't worry about them plates," I say. "I took care of that.
Did you cut yourself on one?"
She bite her lip, look away, and nod.

"Don't you worry about Ella Mae, neither," I say,

untying the scarf.
"She's not welcome in my kitchen."

I stop.
The cut's deep.
And not from no china shard.

"This got anything to do with that Doctor?" I ask.
She don't move,
        but I can tell by her eyes it do.
"Did you see him last night?"
        I can tell by her eyes, she did.
"Did he ... did he hurt you, girl?"
        She shake her head,
        seep them silent tears.

No, it ain't what I feared.
Not yet.

Still, she keeping something from me.

But then,
ain't I been doing the same all these years?

Truth gonna seep out.

"Phoebe, girl," I sigh. Put down my rag.
"I think it time we had a talk."

Different

"Do you know why Ella Mae hate you?
Why she call you 'Yellagirl'?
Why she say you different?"

Phoebe shrug.

"Don't you see?
Your hair,
      it's softer, more brown than black,
your eyes,
      like honey in sunshine,
and your skin,
      lighter than most us slaves,
      and not just field hands."

Phoebe shrug.

"You do look like your momma."

She smile a bit.

"Slender and slight, like her.
Ruthie was beautiful.
But she dark-skinned, like me."

I take Phoebe's hand
and she look at our fingers meshed together,
black-and-tan-and-black-and-tan
She stare like she never seen them before.
Like she trying not to hear what I gotta tell her next.

"Truth is, you *is* different, Phoebe," I say.
"You different because your daddy
is a white man."

To Know

My head pounding with my heart
to hear Ella's words
          coming outta Bea's mouth:

          You is different

to know it true,

to know some white man force himself on my momma,

to know
       what I ain't:
            not black,
            not white,

to wonder
       what I is,

and if that is why
       Momma left me.

Reminders

"I been protecting you for ten years now.
But I see I can't protect you from everything," I say.
"'Specially not the truth.
It's time you know.

"Missus and Ruthie real close once.
They grew up together, just like you and Miss Tessa.
Missus only started hating Ruthie after you was born.
Seven long years she make Ruthie's life hell,
until she finally convinced Master
to sell your momma.

"Missus hate you
'cause you remind her
of your momma.
But she hate you more because
        your soft hair,
        your light skin,
        your honey-eyes,
they remind her

of who your daddy is."

I pause.

"Of what her husband did."

Phoebe's eyes grow wide.

"It's time you know the truth." I hold her hands
even as she raise them to her ears
and shake her head.

"Phoebe," I say, "your daddy
is Master Duncan."

White Lies

"You's still Phoebe.
You's still my little chicken.
You's still Miss Tessa's maid,
and a darn good one," Bea say.
"And you still the apple of Shad's eye."
She smile.
"Nothing changed,
except now you know."

But she wrong.
I's different.
Everything's different.

"I tell you all this now," she say,
"'cause I know that doctor interested in you."

My face burns hot with secrets.

"If he ain't tried something yet,
he will."

Bea grab my shoulders,
make me look her in the eye.
"Listen to me, now.
I been around long enough
to hear a million white lies,
to know:

> White men do what they want,
> with who they want,
> whenever they want.

Never trust a white man, Phoebe.
Stay well away.

They's all want and nothing but trouble."

Heads or Tails

I tell Charlie about the blood drops leading to the clearing.
"And I can't make head nor tail of it."

"Maybe it a rabbit," he say.
"And it drag its bloody self by its two front teeth
to die in its hole."
Maybe. But I ain't seen no burrow.

"Or maybe it a bird.
And the trail end when it fly away. Or a huge hawk eat it."
Maybe. But that too far for an injured bird to hop.
Besides, there were no feathers.

"Maybe it the ghost of that snake charmer," he whisper.
"Folk say he died from the fangs of his five snakes,
and he wander the wood at night
seeking his revenge."

"Sound to me, he don't even know
one end of the snake from the other,"

I say, laughing.
"Besides, they's just stories
to keep the little ones from roaming after dark.
You know that, right?"

Charlie shrug, annoyed.
I know he scared to go out at night.
He fold his arms.
"Sound to me," he say, all sulk and mutter,
"like maybe *you* don't know
one end from the other."

And it hit me:
maybe the ending is the start.
"Charlie," I say, heading for the woods, "you's pretty smart
for a fool."

Smoke and Fire

I's all set to suss that trail again,
when Master see me running by.
"Boy," he say, "get to the barn and replace Ben."

"Yessir, Master," I say
even though I never worked the curing fire before.
But my Master know potential when he see it.

"Mind you keep up with the wood," Benjamin say
before he leave.
Like I don't know how to tend a fire.
My eyes wander the rafters bursting with bundled leaves,
a huge haul of tobacco
just a curing away from going to market.
Green gold, that is.
And Shadrach here be in charge of it.
Master gonna thank me for doing such a great job.
I add log after log
and I watch that flickering flame real close
as the rain tip-tapping on the roof.

I musta close my eyes.
>They stinging so bad.
I musta lay down,
>where the air ain't so hot or smokey.
Not long or nothing.

But that fire musta gone out.

I throws a log in,
but it won't catch what embers is left.

Shadrach, I say.
You got yourself in a heap o' horseshit now.
If there ain't no fire, then there ain't no smoke.
And if there ain't no smoke, then there ain't no curing.
And nobody gonna buy half-baked 'baccy.

And how you think Master gonna thank Shadrach for that?

Count on it

I ain't one to sit around feeling sorry. No, sir.
Alls I need is fire.

I hoof it over to blacksmith's barn,
take a cartload of coal.
It ain't stealing, not really.
I's just moving it from one place to another.

Sweat drip down my face, hiss in the fire pit, as I shovel.
Then I get low
and blow
      and blow
           and blow.

If that fire dead,
I sure is, too.
And I ain't never giving up.
What kinda waste would that be
with all that potential
just sitting in me,

like a barn full of green bundles?

And just when I's about ready to keel over,
red tongues start licking at that coal.

I stay awake all the rest of that night,
heaping on the coal.
'Cause when Shadrach say he gonna do something,
you can count on it.

Options

"What did you do, fool?" Brutus shout,
pulling down a bundle of yellowish leaves.
"You've ruined it. The whole lot!
It ain't s'posed to be yellow!"
He slap me to the ground.

Brutus kick me hard
and go for Master Duncan,
tobacco in hand.
I gots a sickly feeling in my gut
and it ain't from the toe of Brutus's boot.

Now, I admit,
it cross my mind to run for the swamp.
Not forever. Not like Will.
I ain't no fool.
But I get to thinking
maybe Master going to need some time.
I knows where men hide in the mossy glade.
I seen them.

Surely they'd let me stay there
'til Master calmed down.

Head spinning,
stomach churning,
I spends so long kneeling where I fell,
thinking 'bout my options,
that by the time I gets to acting,
Brutus dragging me by the scruff.

And now my only option is
the whipping post.

Morning Lesson

Brutus strip Shad to the waist,
tie his skinny arms around the post,
and walk back a ways,
flexing his muscles,
flicking his whip.

It barely morning,
he only just sound the horn waking workers,
but he gather us round.
'Cause if he teaching someone a lesson,
Brutus want everyone
to watch

and learn.

The First Lash

My hands shaking.
My legs all weak.
I want to be strong,
like Will.
He been whipped three times.

But this is my first.

I want to grit my teeth
and show them all how brave I is.
They watching me.
Phoebe watching me.

But when that whizz-crack come
cross my shoulders,
licking fire down my back,
I cry out
and wet myself.

Like the baby I is.

Four Stripes

Shad got four stripes.
He s'posed to get fifty
only Master himself come into the yard,
tell Brutus to stop.
Poor Shad just dangling from his wrists,
blood dripping down his back
from where the whip bit
crisscross his body
in a w.
The way he cry out,
I know it hurt something awful.
Brutus whipping him like a man.

"What did you do, boy?" Master ask.
Shad raise his eyes. I never seen him look so sorrowful.
Master grab his face.
"What did you do to the fire to make the leaves yellow?"
"I's sorry, Master." Shad crying.
"I musta fall asleep and … and the fire went low."

"Yes, yes, but what did you do next?"
I never seen Master so riled.

Shad quiet for minute.
"I took some of your coal," he say.
"From the blacksmith's."

I bite my lip. Now he done it.
Stealing, too?

S a m e

Master look the same as always:
red hair rimming his freckled head,
vest tight round his barrel belly,
white shirt sleeves rolled and ready for what he gotta do.
He drop Shad's face
and talk to Brutus
while we slaves wait for his word,
or whip—
fearful
like always.

I's glad to see Master look
the same as always.

Nothing
about him seem
anything
like my daddy.

And nothing

about me ever gonna be
anything
like him.

Crazy Man

"Coal!" Master say, "Don't you see? That's it—coal!"

He whoop and holler like a crazy man.
Even Missus look concerned
when he run to the fire pit nearby,
set the tip of that leaf ablaze,
wave it under her nose.

"Smell it, Maggie, smell it!" Master shout,
as she cough and wave her hand.
"That, my dear, is the smell of success!"

But it just burnt tobacco,
if you ask me.

Investors Meeting

Gentlemen, I give you: Whitehaven Gold Leaf Tobacco.
The cream of our crop.
    Our last hope.
A charcoal-cured tobacco, like nothing you've ever seen.
Or tasted.
Revolutionary.
    Accidental.
Imagine a leaf that's brighter. Milder.
Imagine a smoke you inhale.
Surely fortifying.
    Probably poisonous.
And I've got six hundred pounds of it
hanging in my rafters.
A limited supply.
    My last harvest.
And enough eager buyers
to sell it for a price that's reasonable.
    Outrageous.
What's more, no one knows the recipe but me.
    And the boy.

Lucky Pup

Ever since he make a mess of that crop a week back,
Shad been the Master's pup,
trotting at his heels,
begging for attention,
doing any trick
for Master's praise and prize.

Shad prance around like he invented yellow leaf
on purpose.
We all know
he just lucky.
And luck has a way of running out,

eventually.

New Clothes

Shad forget about his whipping,
about his wetting and weeping.
Shad even forget about Will and Charlie.
And this morning, when Bea ask him where the milk at
and he say, "Get a Quarter boy to do it,"
I knows Shad surely forget hisself.

"I did not hear that coming outta your fool mouth,"
Bea cuff him,
kick him to the door.
"You still my kitchen boy.
Now, get your sorry ass down to the stables
and bring me that milk
or you can tell Missus yourself why her tea is still black."
Bea toss him down the steps.
Slam the door.
"Fancy pants and new shoes
don't change the fool that wearing them," she say.

And she right.

I know it. She know it.

But Shad sure don't.

Thanks to Me

I heard Master say Gold Leaf Tobacco saved Whitehaven.

Thanks to me.

Without Gold Leaf,
Bea, Phoebe, all y'all Whitehaven slaves
woulda been on the auction block.
But do any of you thank me?
No, sir. Not a one.

This must be how poor Master Duncan feel,
carrying all you ungrateful Negroes.

Except for me. I's grateful.
"Thank you, Master," I say. "Oh, thank you, sir."
          when he give me my new clothes,
          when he invite me to move my pallet from
          the stables to the Big House,
          when he say he gonna be keeping
a real close eye on me.

Bea can't boss me no more.

I'm gonna talk to Master about my plans.

For me. For Phoebe.

Yessir, lots of things gonna be happening 'round here,

thanks to me.

The Least I Can Do

No one else sells Gold Leaf.
No one else can cure it.
No one else knows my secret:
that coal is key.

That boy saved his skin
and mine
by stoking that fire last week.
Any idiot could've fallen asleep in the curing barn.
But Shadrach's the idiot that did.
Either way, I figured I'd get the boy some new clothes.
Ones that fit.

It's the least I can do.

But he's getting too big for his britches now, asking:
to apprentice with Sam
to marry Phoebe
to have his own cabin.
I'll admit, the boy has initiative,

and that's what scares me.
Perhaps he's more like his brother than I thought.
So I'm keeping a close eye on him.
He can ask all he wants,
but if he even thinks about telling
my secret—
he's done.

I'll cut out his tongue before I let him breathe a whisper.

That is the least I will do.

Smoke and Mirrors

Doctor Bergman's not impressed by
the richness of Daddy's smoke
or how I primp in Mother's mirrors.

Breathtaking, I was,
at our big dinner
and he barely noticed
with all that talk of crops and flocks.

I'm tired of doing things Mother's way,
with her floppy hats
and fancy meals
and foolish orchids.
I've been a simpering fool.

I know what men really want.

So I'll show him what I have.
I'll give him what he wants
to get what I am after.

For once the deed is done,
he'll have to marry me.

Bedtime

Miss Tessa tell me not to braid her hair for bed.
She wear it loose and long.
Miss Tessa tell me to put back her cotton nightie.
Fetch her silk robe instead.
The way she pinching her cheeks
and putting on pearls and perfume,
you think she's going a-courtin'

and not a-climbin' into that canopy bed.

Secrets

Secrets got a way of keeping you up at night,
scuttling in the corners of your mind,
weaving webs of worry under your eyes.

My mind crawling with them,
itching while I lay helpless.

They meeting at Carson's Corners tomorrow.
> *Is Birdman an abo-li-tion-ist?*
> *Ain't they criminals come to steal us away?*
> *And what if he lying?*
> *Even if he telling the truth—what if Will run?*
> *What if he get caught again?*

> *Should I tell Shad?*

Miss Tessa's door click open
and I wait for her
to call me,
to scold me,

to tell me what she want.
But she don't.

Instead, she tiptoe past me
down the dark hall
to Birdman's door.
And without even knocking,
she crank the handle real slow
and let herself in.

Seems like she gots some secrets of her own.

Playing with Fire

He leans over his desk,
a clutter of sketchbooks and notes,
writing in the flickering candlelight.
So intent on what he pens,
he hasn't heard me enter
or walk up behind him
to brush the broad shoulders that pull his shirt so taut.
My touch makes him jump,
spill black ink across the page,
as he bolts to his feet to face me.
"Miss Tessa?"

"Ross," I smile, let him look at me
standing in my robe.

"Miss Tessa!" he gasps, breathless,
glances at the door.
"What are you doing here?"

My hands slither up his chest

and he grabs them,
forcefully,
making my heart race even more.

I smile. "You know why I'm here."

Burning

"This is ridiculous ..." he whispers.
"Your father would ..."

I kiss him then,
sure it will make him forget my father,
the letter,
those damned birds.
Sure the burning want will make him forget everything
but me,
leave him weak-limbed and woozy
like Johnny Cooke was.
Like I am now.

But it doesn't.

"Stop." He pulls back, shoves me away.
I try again.
"Enough." He scolds me like a parent,
weary with my childish games,
then turns back to his desk.

"I think you should go."

But …
My shame burns like the candle's flame:
hot, intense, and illuminating.
Why wouldn't he want me?
Any available man would.
         Unless …

He flips his sketchbook face down on his letter,
but not before I see a glimpse of truth.
A sketch, not of birds, but

a woman.

First Time

Moments after she go in,
Miss Tessa bolt outta that door
and come flying down the hall,
robe flapping,
tears flowing.
She throw herself on her bed
and sob her sorry self to sleep.

I smile in the dark.

Look like Miss Tessa didn't get what she want.
I guess there's a first time
for everything.

Her

Phoebe brings me breakfast in bed the next morning.
I can't face him, not after last night.
Not with these puffy eyes.

Another woman.
Of course that's why. It all makes sense now.

My shame had subsided somewhat,
but not my curiosity.
She must be something special for him
to choose Her over me.
Who was this mystery woman?
And why hadn't he mentioned Her?

Throwing off the covers, I set the tray aside
and tiptoe down the hall,
as voices echoed from below,
spoons clinking on teacups.
Another ten minutes, at least.

I retrace my steps into his room,
to his desk,
now empty of all but an ink stain.
His packed bags sit on his bed—
he's leaving today.
but I know that sketchbook will be in his satchel.
And it is.
I open it,
flip past birds and nests and weeds,
to the very back
to the ink-stained page,
to where he'd sketched Her:

... Phoebe?

Mother Said

"Look what I found."
I hand the sketch to Mother
but keep last night to myself.
She looks at me suspiciously
but I press on, like she would.
You've got to believe your story
if you want others to.
"I suppose he forgot *that* was in his notebook
when he loaned it to me."

"Didn't I tell you?" Mother complains.
"She's nothing but trouble.
Get rid of her, I said to him when she was born.
Get rid of her, I said when he finally sold Ruth.
But, no, no one listens to me.
And here we are."

My eyes burn from memory's sting. "How could Doctor—"

"Oh, forget him. Our fortunes have changed,

and there's a thousand more suitable suitors,
never you worry."
She sits and stares in the mirror at me,
at us.
She seems old.
Tired.
As though my discovery deflates her, too.

"Men are selfish, my girl.
They're all the same.
It won't matter which one you marry,
whoever steals your heart
is sure to break it."
She stares off, eyes wet and weary,
as though great hurt lies beneath her hate.
I'd never seen her so frail.
She blinks twice and turns to me,
her fire feeble,
but her words a warning,
a plea more compelling than any demand:

"I beg you, child, for your own good,
one woman to another:

 Get rid of Phoebe."

Leaving

Master shake Birdman's hand,
give him a box of Gold Leaf smokes.
"The cream of Whitehaven's crop," he say.
"Take them and tell your Northern friends all about us."

Birdman say he surely will.

"Tessa sends her farewell, she's feeling under the weather,"
Master tell him,
"brokenhearted that you're going, I'd say."

"Arnold!" Missus scold.
She look at Birdman. "So, Doctor,
did you ever find your elusive … bird?"

Birdman say he surely did.

He look at me, eyes full of secrets.
Missus watch me sideways.
She know something.

But what?

Birdman climb up in his wagon,
tip his hat,
slap the reins
and get to leaving.
Wheels crunch on the gravel
as it slowly roll down the long lane of tall trees
to life outside of Whitehaven.

To where I never been.

Strange

"Nice fellow." I watch the doctor drive away.
"Strange, though."
I'd told him his future was here for the taking.
He could have had Tessa's hand.
He could have had Whitehaven
one day.

But he said he had work to do
today
to drive south;
"to draw birds."

I shake my head as he disappears over the horizon
leaving nothing behind but a dust cloud.

"He may be a wealthy scholar,
but I'd say he's birdbrained."

Bird Brained

I used to think Master know'd everything.
But he never know'd:
>   why Birdman came
>   what Birdman said
>   who Birdman is.

He right about one thing, though,
Birdman is birdbrained.

Birdman a watcher,
>   like the sharp-eyed chickadee;

he a hawk-hunter,
>   bold enough to swoop and steal
>   right outta your nest;

and he can mockingbird-mimic
>   well enough to fool any old bird,

>   even the Master hisself.

Noticed

Later that afternoon, I sit on the porch and watch Phoebe
hang the sheets out back,
hauling her wet-heavy wash on her hip,
leaning and lugging
from basket to line with her strong arms.

I've seen her do it a million times.
And yet—
I'd never noticed
      she's taller,
      still slender,
            but not the gangly girl I knew.
I never saw the
      curves of breast and bottom
      that swell above and below
      the knotted apron strings
      tied tight around her narrow waist.
Until now.

She stoops and stands.

Curls fall free from her tightly bound bun,
dangling from her kerchief in perfect spirals
dark against her slender nape—
her beauty spilling out.

These past few years,
I'd been so busy fussing over my looks,
I hadn't noticed hers.

But Ross had.
Any man would.

Mine

"Daddy ..."
Tessa comes into my study and she's after something:
a new dress, another horse.
She knows I'd give her anything she wants.
"... I want to sell Phoebe."

Anything
but that.

"Does she work hard?" I ask.
        Tessa nods.
"Obedient?"
        She nods again.
"Do you want Brutus to discipline her?
A few lashes is often all it takes to make them—"

"I just don't want her anymore." She pouts.
"Does there have to be a reason?"

The suddenness of it surprises me.

But then, you can't make sense of a woman's whim.
Sighing,
I dip the nib, write the numbers, sign my name.
"Five hundred dollars," I hold out the check.
"That's more than she's worth."

Tessa ignores it, arms folded, cheeks flushed,
the spit of her mother making demands.
"You gave her to me, Daddy. I own her.
She's mine. Can't I do as I please?"

She's right. The girl is hers by law.

But mine by blood.

Daughter

I look at the check.
Five hundred dollars?
He must be joking.
"She's worth double that, and you know it."

Daddy glares at me,
and for a moment I feel like I'm five years old.
Then he smiles. "You're your father's daughter.
A Duncan, through and through."
He writes another for a thousand. "My final offer."

But he's wrong. I'm not all Duncan.
I am my mother's daughter, too.

"Daddy," I say, "I can read the papers.
Men pay close to two thousand for a girl like Phoebe."
I pause.
"A fancy girl."

Daddy's mouth opens, but he doesn't speak.

I suppose it's news to him
that his baby knows the way of things.
He clears his throat. Shuffles papers.
"I told your mother
nothing good comes out of women reading."

"Four maids for the price of one," I say,
appealing to his business side.
"Give me one good reason
why I shouldn't sell her?"

And I know by the way he blusters and shuffles,
he can't.

Master's Mood

After dinner, I clear the table
and bring Master his cigar box,
like always.
Only this time, he just wave me away,
like he annoyed I brought it.
And when I gets his whiskey,
like always,
he get up and leave
without taking no sip
or saying no word to nobody.

Even Old Sam look at me funny.

Master in some kind of mood tonight.

I wonder what got him so riled.
Whatever it is,
Missus and Miss Tessa know.
That's why they's still
gloating.

Study

Miss Tessa shut me out,
say she can dress herself for bed.
That true. But in all our long years together,
she never done it once.
Maybe she know I seen her running from Birdman's room.
Maybe she embarrassed.

Bea tell me to snuff the lantern in the study,
But Master ain't abed—
he passed out in his leather chair.
Whiskey, by the smell of it.
I fetch Old Sam and together we heave him to his feet.

"Ruth?" Master say, his eyes and words all blurry.
"I'm sorry, Ruth." He grip my hand. "I'm so sorry."
He start crying then.

"Master," Sam say like he talking to a child,
"Ruth gone ten years now, remember?
Sold away."

But it don't help none.
In fact it make him worse.
"But I don't want to sell her," Master say,
squeezing my hand like he never gonna let go.
"I promised I wouldn't. I promised, Sam. She's mine."

"Come on, sir."
Sam put Master's arm around his shoulders,
ease him away from me.
"Time for bed.
Everything gonna look better in the morning.
It always does."

Four Letters

Master's red leather book lie where he left it on his desk
spread to some middle page,
but not just any page—
Momma's page.
Wasn't he just thinking about the day he sold her,
wishing he hadn't?
I glance at the door.
And lean over the book,
running my finger run down long rows of letters,
looking for four: *r-u-t-h*

My heart stop.

April 10, 1847   Ruth.   Sold to John Scott, North Carolina

I did it, Momma.
I watched. I learned. I saved up words
and finally found where you went.

But now what?

So what if I can read
her name
or where she sold?
She ten years gone now.
Maybe even sold again and again since then.

I slump in the chair.

What good it do—to read, to know, to hope?

It don't change nothing.
Momma's still gone.

One Letter

Finding those four letters don't change nothing, really.
But then I sees one letter that do.

It drying on his desk
ink wet with what he wrote.
The page tremble in my hands,
but it nothing to the trembling inside
as I sound out word by word:

for sale
16-year-old
Mu-la-tto maid.
Hard wor-king
mute.
Young and like-ly.
Suit-able bree-der,
La-dy's maid,
or fan-cy girl.
Goes by "Phoe-be."
$1500.

And just like how letters make words,
it all come together:
>Why Master crying.
>Why Missus gloating.
>Why Tessa shut me out.

Even as he sold my momma away,
Master musta promised her he'd never sell me.
After all,
>what kind of man sell his own child?

Just goes to show,
you can't never trust
a white man's word.

Dry Wood

"Fetch me some firewood, boy," Bea say.
       Like I's fresh from the field
       and not the Master's
       right-hand man's right hand.
"Dry wood, you hear?" she nag.
       Like I don't know.
"And don't skimp, neither."
       Like I do.

Ax in the wagon, I grumble deep in the forest,
kicking deadwood along the trail.
Most logs and limbs laying in the damp grass
too wet to burn.
But my mind as sharp as this here blade,
'cause straightaways it cut to where I seen
perfect firewood:
a tall hollow husk of it,
enough to fill this whole wagon.
And it just waiting for me

in the clearing.

Nuts and Seeds

Squirrels know
a hollow tree
got enough hidey holes to hold
their secret stash
of nuts and seeds.

But as that old stump in the clearing
crack and split
beneath my blade,
what spill out

ain't acorns.

And no squirrel I ever seen
keep nuts in a jar,
or notes in a book,
or a burlap bag of tools.

Looks like somebody
been squirreling away
seeds of trouble.

Looks like squirrels
ain't the only ones with
autumn plans.

Day of Rest

Sunday is a day of rest, Master always says.
My slaves don't work.
Well, not in the fields, anyhow.

On Sunday, field hands
     mend clothes;
     clean cabins;
     hoe collard;
     pick peas and taters
     outta their secret gardens.
They get ready for the week,
     beating hominy in the pot;
     grinding corn for hoecakes;
     fishing;
     fetching turtles;
     hunting rabbit, coon, or possum.
Even I got more work on a Sunday,
     making pies and pastries,
     roasting like that big old bird in the oven
     while I make Master's Sunday dinner.

No. Slaves get no rest.
Sunday just like any other day—they all the same.

Except, of course, for Saturday nights. They's our own.

Most Saturday Nights

Most Saturday nights,
couples go courting in the Quarter.
Girls tie on a ribbon,
  if they got one,
give it to their sweetheart,
  if they got one.

Most Saturday nights,
everyone, young and old, come
to dance on dirt floors,
to forget the week of work behind
and before us.

Most Saturday nights,
Levi play the fiddle,
Will beat the pans,
Ella Mae tap the tambourine,
and Shad slap his thighs and stomp his feet,
brag he patting juba better than anyone else.

Most Saturday nights,
Bea and me go down to the Quarter.
I clap. And smile.
And dance with Shad.

But tonight be different
than most.

Come midnight, those boys are gonna run.
Come tomorrow, they be gone.
Come next Saturday, I be sold.

And I can't do nothing about it.

My Best Friend

Smiling,
Shad take me in his arms,
and spin me 'round the floor,
but his eye on Will.

Shad is my best friend, I think.
Maybe I should tell him
          this be the last time
                    he hear his brother sing,
          the last time
                    we dance.

But I don't.

Shad can't do nothing neither.
So I let him dance and have his fun,
I let him think this is just like

most Saturday nights

because
Shad
is my best friend.

A Sliver of Hope

Under the sliver moon,
Phoebe and I walk back to the Big House.
The secret I's carrying so heavy on my shoulders,
I can't bear it no more.
But if anyone can keep it,
my Phoebe can.

"I think Will gonna run again," I whisper.

She stop, look at me, eyes wide in the dark.

"I found a bag hidden in the hollow tree,
and a knife, money, a brass dial, and a gun.
Someone's planning to run, Phoebe," I say.
"It's gotta be Will."

She shake her head.
She can't believe it neither.

"I won't let him leave me." My jaw tightens.

"So I hid the bag in the barn,
in an empty Gold Leaf barrel.
But I gave Master the book of writing.
I can't read it—but he sure will."

Phoebe grip my arm then.
I can tell she terrified.

"Don't worry," I say, hand on her shoulder.
"I took care of it. Will won't run without his things.
Meanwhile Master gonna find out
who been leading my brother astray."

I breathe a sigh of relief.
It feels good to get it out,
to know I did the right thing,
to have a sliver of hope.
My hand brushes down Phoebe's arm
across a thick scab.
She winces and pulls away.

I ask: "What happened—"

but she's already gone,
running in the shadows.

Truth

I run until my heart bursting.
Until my head spinning.
Until I can't run no more.
But it don't change nothing.

You can't run from the truth.

Shad know about Will's secret.
He might even tell Master.
And Master know:
      someone been reading and writing,
      someone hiding it from him,
      someone about to get peeled and pickled.
He might even know that someone
      is me.

Master smart. He gonna know them words is mine.
He knows my secret.
I can't run from truth.
But the truth is,

now that it's out,

running might be the only choice.

Bold

"Tessa," Daddy asks, barging into my room, "is this yours?"
He thrusts the notebook at me,
the one I tossed in the trash two tutors ago.
My bold protest.

"Daddy, that was a long time—"

"Is this your writing?" he asks.

I take it, flip through the first pages of my early scrawls,
stopping at a new hand.
"It's my book—but those aren't my words."
The writing is faint, childish at first,
strengthening as the pages progress
from letters to words.
a - b - c
cat
cook
momma
warbler

I turn the page and glance at Daddy.
I know why he's riled.
He should be.

"I didn't write this," I say, "but I know who did."
I point to one word
printed over and over and over,
its line growing
strong
and bold:

feebee

Whole Truth

Master still up when I get in.
"Tell me again where you found this?" he say.

So I do.
But I don't say nothing about the bag.
Or Will.

"One of my slaves is keeping secrets from me,
learning to read and write," he say.
"I don't suppose you know anything about it?"

"No, sir," I say. "I found it and brought it to you
straightaways.
I can't read, Master. That's against the law."

He eyeball me,
size me up like a bundle of 'baccy.
Sussing if I telling true.
And I can hold his eye, 'cause I am.
Shad always speaks the truth,

Just not all of it.

"You know who it is?" I ask.
I need to know who in cahoots with Will.
He nod, but he don't speak the name.
Still it don't matter none.
Come morning, I'll know. We all will.
When Brutus strap that sorry slave to the post
and gather us 'round,
we all gonna see who been bad
and Will finally gonna see sense.

That broken body coulda been his, but it ain't
because of me.

"Go on, then. Get some sleep," Master finally say.
"In the morning, I'll deal with Phoebe."

My stomach drop.
> *That Phoebe's book?*
> *My Phoebe's reading and writing?*
> *Why didn't she tell me?*
> *Why didn't she trust me?*
It hurts me to know the truth she shared with me
ain't whole neither.

But it kills me to think that broken body gonna be hers,
because of me.

What I Know

When the house dark, I tiptoe in the back door,
sure my thumping heart gonna wake them.
But the kitchen empty.
Bea ain't here to protect me,
Miss Tessa ain't here to command me,
And Shad ain't here to distract me
from what I gotta do.

Only I don't know what that is,
just yet.

My pallet wait upstairs outside Miss Tessa's door.
It would be so easy to lie down, like always,
waiting 'til someone tells me what I gotta do.

But I think of Will and the boys.
Will gonna see the tree and bag gone,
and his hopes with them.
He already tried running without a compass
and he didn't get very far.

And if Master learn they's running,
that knife and gun might be what save them
from the hounds' teeth.

And only I knows how to get it to them.

Keeping Her

There's one more thing I gotta do,
in case the next thing be the last.
I sneak into the dining room,
carry Yellowbird's cage to the kitchen counter.
It don't matter that I keep her food coming
and her cage clean,
or that I keep her safe from Rufus.

Sure, I keep her alive,
but I's keeping her
from living like a yellow bird should.

Unlatching the metal door, I reach in,
but she don't tremble,
don't fuss and flutter,
even in my cupped hands.
Miss Tessa said the bird is tame.
Tame just another word for broke.
Her wing is long healed.
But numbed by what life she knows behind those bars,

Yellowbird stopped hoping for one beyond them.
Truth is,
that cage is hurting her in ways I can't fix.
I keep her alive,
but she's living half-dead.
And it just ain't right.
I know it in my bones.

I carry Yellowbird to the back stoop,
but even when I open my hands,
she don't fly into that unknown.

Like her momma,
I know she ain't mine to keep.
So, like her momma,
I toss her out.
Against everything in me that say not to—
I throw her at the dark and all its dangers.
She fall and swoop, a streak of yellow in the night,
landing on the empty trough out back.
She rustle her bright wings,
cock her head at me,
then that feathered hope make for the trees—

sweet-sweet-sweet-life-so-sweet!

singing at last,
like a yellow bird should.

Tracking Truth

Phoebe got herself in a heap of trouble now,
keeping her secret book from Master and me.
I stare at the fire in the curing barn,
blind to what's right in front of me,
my mind tracking a trail of lies
running circles 'round that stump
       where we had our secret kiss,
       where she hid her secret words,
       where I found those secret tools.

Did she know about the bag, too?
Should Master?
Maybe it's time to tell the whole truth.

But Phoebe's book wasn't in the bag.
Maybe she isn't part of the plan.
Surely she would have told me,
if she knew about Will wanting to run.
No. She don't know nothing about
no dial or money, no gun or knife.

Heck, if Phoebe had a gun,
she'd likely shoot herself in the foot.
And if Phoebe had a knife, she'd—

my heart stop.

The scab.
The blood from stump to well.
I see her, then,
my Phoebe
at the end of the trail,
arm cut deep by the knife

dripping proof.

What I Have to Do

Wind whistles through the barn,
rattling dead leaves in the rafters.
Through the split board,
I see Shad shovel coal on the fire and sit back on a barrel.
I know then,
which one holds Will's bag,
what I have to do.

Pitching pebbles, I rustle the bushes over yonder.
And just like I knew he would, Shad come skulking,
looking to catch who's sneaking,
looking to make Master proud.

While he gone,
I slip in and open that barrel and snatch the bag.
But before I can bolt,
Shad's footsteps crunch up the path.

I grab Shad's shovel and scoop the fire,
heave embers into the bushels overhead,

then hunker behind the casks,
heart pounding as he come in.

Shad look at the shovel I left lying.
Look in the barrel I left empty.
Throwing down the lid, he look my way
and I's left cornered as he step toward me.

A crackling-snap make him look up
to where smoky leaves whoosh into a blaze above.
And just like I knew he would,
Shad run for the rain barrel.
Bag in hand, I run, too.

Shad's fate depend on them bundles.
Just like Will's depend on this here bag.
I hope he understand.
I hope he forgive me, someday,

for what I have to do.

I Don't Know

Skirts hiked, I cut through the dark field,
leaves lashing at my legs.
But it don't matter. If Master catch me now,
I be whipped worse than by tobacco blades.
Much worse.

I don't know
if Will and the boys gonna be at Carter's Corners.
Maybe they got scared when they saw their bag gone.
Maybe they decided not to run.

I don't know
if Birdman gonna come.
Maybe Shad gonna tell.
Maybe Master gonna show.

I don't even know what happens
after I bring this bag to Carter's Corners.

I just know that I have to.

I stop at the edge of the field,
at the edge of my world,
scared 'cause I don't know nothing about nothing
past Whitehaven's fence.
But I think of Will and Joe and Davey and Levi
and I climb,
rung by rung,
swing my leg over
the fence
and jump down on the other side.
Heart racing,
I swallow,

take a step,

and another.

Each terrifying
one
      taking
            me
                 the
                      farthest
                         I
                            ever
                               been.

Fire

Water splash up in the rafters,
killing that fire and the one below
to a hissing smoke.
Them burnt bundles ain't nothing but wet mulch now.
I kick the coals and wonder if it worth starting another fire.
If there's anything left saving.

I know it was Phoebe.

I seen her shadow running cross the far field
racing for the river, bag in hand.
I know what she did.

But I'll never know why.

I had plans for us. Big plans.
But all them dreams gone up in flames
and I's left alone.
Left here to put it out.
To pay.

Master oughta know. He gonna.

He'll be some fired up,
but I'll kindle that blaze,
'cause I think my brother and my girl,
they's worth saving.
And when Master bring them back
and learn them a lesson,
maybe he can make them finally see sense.

Lord knows, I can't.

The Route

Shad fishes at Carter's Corners,
so I follow the creek.
Sure enough, that winding water lead me
right to where the rivers meet.
But there ain't a soul around.

Heart pumping, I move tree to tree
up to the crossroads,
scanning the ditches for their shadows.

Maybe they ain't here.
Maybe they ain't running.
Maybe I just burned bundles,
burned bridges,
for nothing.

A whole lot of maybes
but one thing's for sure:

I's in a mess of trouble.

Crossroads

I could go to Master and confess,
tell him I's sorry I been hiding my learning,
sorry I burned his crop of bundles,
sorry I walked away from Whitehaven.
Master might show mercy to his mulatto-girl.

But I doubt it.

If I go back,
he just whip me in ways that won't show
when he sell me
away from Whitehaven.

I crouch at the crossroads
in a ditch of dread,
listening for men I can't see,
wondering if a wagon gonna come,
knowing whatever I choose
takes me away from Whitehaven—
from what I know.

Too scared to go back,
too lost to move ahead.
I can do nothing but
cower in the dark.

Bird's Eye View

What now, Momma?

Listen to the birds, she'd always say.

And she right.
Birds know how to build a home anywhere,
straw by straw.
Birds know how to forage and feed
wherever they find theyselves.
But most of all,
birds know when it's time to fly on.

How'd they know? I asked her,
as we watched a flock fly north.
An arrow in the sky.

The good Lord gave them will and wings to fly.
All they gotta do is
listen
and leap.

So I listen. But I don't hear nothing.
Not even no owl nor whippoorwill.
The wood strangely silent.

And I smile then,
in the blind dark.
'Cause I know what birds know;
what they see;
why they's silent.

Someone else here, somewhere,
hiding in the ditches,
Listening for wagon wheels,
waiting to leap.

Wagon

A wagon come rolling up the road,
rumbling like thunder in the silence.
It pass where I huddle in the ditch
but it don't stop.
A lone driver sit hunched over,
in his dark coat,
wide-brimmed hat hiding his eyes.
Them farmer's clothes,
that smooth-skinned jaw,
don't look like the bearded Birdman I know'd.

He haul the reins a ways up and stop,
listening.

I don't know the signal.
But he's not moving.
Nobody is.

Maybe he a paddyroller
patrolling at night to catch and punish

slaves on the loose.

Slaves like me.

The Call

coo-WOO   woo-woo-woo

a dove echoes eerie in the dark,
shivering my spine.
I listen to its soulful song.
But mourning doves ain't nightbirds.
You never hear them call, come dark.
Except for once ...
when I's hiding in the tree.

coo-WOO   woo-woo-woo

It call again—
and know it him.
It Birdman.

So I leap.

Out of the Shadows

Four shadows creep outta the ditches next to the wagon:
Will and the others.
They's there, just like them silent birds said.

I run up the road, sack in hand.
"Phoebe?" Will whisper as I draw near.
"What the hell you doing here?"
I hold up the bag as the men clamber into the wagon bed.

"She stole our bag!" Levi say.

I shake my head. But here I come, holding it.

"You tell on us?" Levi ask,
but it don't matter what I say,
his answer thunders up the road behind me:

Master and Brutus,
armed and angry,
coming all hoof and hellfire.

Right

She running for the crossroads, Master, I said.
That's where they must be meeting.

Master heed me.
Haul me up behind him when I say,
I knows a shortcut.
Me and Master gallop through the dark,
alongside Brutus.
Shackles clanking in saddlebags.
Guns cocked.
Ropes wrapped and ready to haul them home.

And as we round the corner I see
Will,
the wagon,
and Phoebe running red-handed to meet them.

"Well done, Shadrach!"
Master say the words I long to hear
as he spur his horse on.

"You were right!"

Only this time,
it don't feel so good to know it.

Underestimated

She's running for the wagon,
as it pulls away,
men cowering in the bed.

I never knew the dumb girl had it in her
        to read and write
        to learn and lie
        to burn my stores and steal my slaves.

A will of iron grit, she has,
and the wisdom to hide it well.
More Duncan than I thought.
More dangerous, too.

I rein in,
raise my revolver.
Hold her in my sights:
        Ruth's girl.
        Mine.
I'll do what I have to.

To keep order. To keep control.
I'll shoot her in the back
before I let her sneak behind mine again.

Running

I reach for Levi's hand as I race,
hoping he'll haul me over the sideboards.
But a shot explode behind me
as he take the bag.
And just like that,

Levi's head burst
like a firecracker in a pumpkin
and he tumble out of the wagon.

Birdman's horses surge ahead, spooked by the sound
and I keep running.
Running.
Running.
Even as
the drumming hooves and jangling chains
of Master's men
come closer and closer.

I try not to hear them.

try not to feel the pain in my side,
the cramps in my legs,
try not to think of poor Levi
left dead in the ditch.

Else I'll be next.

Will stretch out his hand,
risking his hide for mine.
"Come on, Phoebe!" he yell. "You can do it!"

Running toward Will.
Running from Master.
Running for my life.

Only I don't know if I can run much longer.

One Shot

My ears ring from the blast of his gun,
heart ringing with truth:
     Master gonna kill them.
He ain't looking to learn them lessons.
It revenge, plain and simple.

And I wonder if that why I's here, too.

"Take them!" He give me the reins,
hold his gun in both hands,
steadying himself as he look down the barrel
at my brother
reaching for my girl's hand.

Master cocks the hammer.
If he shoots now
he can take them both with one bullet
before they run away from me
for good.

One shot
to stop it—
is all I have.

And I take it.

Take the Reins

I pull back on those reins
with everything I got.
Master's horse wheels hard left
just as Master about to shoot.

I pull the reins.
Master take his shot.
And Brutus, riding on our left side,
take that bullet
right to his chest.

Right to his grave.

Enough

Birdman's horses race ahead at the crack of the gun,
pulling Will's fingertips further and further from mine.

I push from my toes.
Pump with my arms.
I reach with all I got left in me.
But all I got

ain't enough.

Tripping,
　　　　I tumble
　　　　　　　to a
　　　　　　　　　　stop.

Sprawled in the middle of the road,
scuffed, scraped, and grazed by gravel,
gasping for air and heaving with heartache
in the wagon's wake of dust and pebble,
I watch it escape—

without me.

Kicking the Stars

Master's horse rears up on the road behind,
front legs kicking,
grasping at the stars
as it whinnies and falls back
on its riders—
          on Master
          on Shad.

The horse get up.

But no one else do.

Broken

I run for where Shad lie
broke from the fall,
his legs all bent in ways they won't,
his head, too heavy for his neck.
'Minding me of that baby bird
all feeble, frail, and flung from its nest.

"Phoebe?" he say, voice cracking,
like his heart more broke than his bones.
"Why you leaving me?"

And I look at
my friend Shad,
through all the secrets and betrayals
that come between us,
to where he lie—
gun on one side.
Master on the other.

Within Reach

Master struggles to his feet.
He can't walk on that broken ankle
but that don't stop him from hobbling closer.
I step away,
out of Master's reach,
and look back
at the wagon long gone.

"She's going to bolt, Shadrach.
I see it in her eye," Master say,
all grimace and grit as he shuffle toward me.
"Get the gun; hold her for me."

And Shad,
my Shad,
do.

He pick up the Master's gun next to him.
He cock the hammer where he lie.
He turn that black barrel on me,

the girl
> who lost him his brother;
> who cost him his legs;
> who broke his heart.

"Don't move," he say to me,
his voice trembling
like his lips,
like that gun.
"You ain't going nowhere but home, Phoebe."

And Master smile.

Sure Thing

Shad might let me go.
Or he might pull the trigger.

But Master?
He's a sure thing.
Master gonna keep coming 'til he get me.
And when he do,
he'll surely make me pay.

I take a step back.

"Don't!" Shad shout.

But I take another.
One eye on Shad where he lie in the dirt
and the other on Master,
who so close now I can smell his sweat.

"Shoot her!" Master shout. "Do it!"

From Me

I think my legs is broken.
But I don't feel a thing
except the weight of this gun.

"Do it!" Master say.
And I always do what Master say.

But then I looks at my Phoebe backing away
like she's got somewheres else to go.

*Why you wanna run
from me?*

Master getting closer to her.
But she's keeping out of reach.
"Shoot her, Shadrach," he say. "In the leg.
Or she'll get away—
from me."
I look at his sweaty face, his crazy eyes.

He's right.

"What about your plans?" he say. "Your cabin. Your wife.
You have to make her mind you, boy.
Or she never will."

Master right about that, too.

"Do it," he say. "Pull the trigger."

I look at Phoebe.
At her leg.
And wonder:
    How we gonna dance if I shoot it?
And know:
    We never will if I don't.

Eyes torn
between my Master and my Phoebe.
Heart torn
'cause I can't give them both what they want
from me.

Reeling In

"Do it," I say, "... and I'll make you overseer."

Shadrach's mouth drops like a gaping cod's.
He's taking it hook, line, and sinker.

Another few words and I've got him.
Another few steps and I've got her.
Either way,
I win.

"Brutus is dead," I say, steeling his resolve
as he sets his sights on power and position.
On Phoebe's leg.
He closes one eye.

"The job is yours," I say.
"Are you man enough?"

Decision Made

Shad gets that look he always do
right before he leap.
Lips tightened.
Head raised.
Decision made.

He gonna shoot me.

But this time,
I made a decision
of my own.

"Don't," I say,
speaking my secret words,
voice cracking like a speckled shell,
"please, Shad."

Gospel Truth

I near drop the gun when I hear her,
my Phoebe, saying my name,
begging me not to shoot.

"You can talk?" I say.

She nods.

"Why you never talk before?"

"I never had nothing to say."
Her voice a whisper.
"Nobody gonna listen anyhow."

"Why you running away?" I ask. "The truth, now."

"I ain't Master's shame," she say,
eyes puddled up with tears.
"I ain't Tessa's toy,
or even your girl, Shad."

She shrug.
"I's Phoebe. Just Phoebe. I belong to no one."

"You're mine!" Master growl, stumbling closer.
Making Phoebe step back.
Making me raise the gun.

She look at me.
"No matter how many Masters say it,
or pastors preach it,
or how many long years we be living like this—"

With every word, her voice grows stronger,
my gun, heavier.

"—owning people is wrong,
shameful wrong, Shad.
And that's the gospel truth."

At Least

While Phoebe speaking,
Master lunge and snatch her.

At least I don't have to shoot her now.
At least she's caught and coming home.

Master raise his hand,
slap her head and face,
make her cringe and cry out,
cowering beneath her skinny arms.
She deserve it for all she done.

But he don't let up.

"I'm going to whip the skin off you myself," he yell.
"Lying, good for nothing girl!
You think you can steal my slaves?
Burn my crops?
Lie to me?"

Phoebe's face bleeding now.
Eyes rolling.
Arms falling.
He beating her real bad.

"Stop!" I yell from where I lie, helpless in the dirt.
"Stop, Master!"

He glare at me. "Shut your mouth, boy!"

"I'll do it!" I say,
knowing a whipping from me wouldn't kill her.
"Ain't it my job?"

He laugh. "Did you really think I'd make you overseer,
you dumb fool?
You haven't the nerve to even fire a gun."
He look me over. "Besides, you'll never walk again.
You're even more useless than you were before."

"But this one," he drag Phoebe over to his horse,
"I'll chain her by the ankles,
like her high and mighty mother,
stand her naked on the auction block,
until she's bought and broke by the highest bidder."
He pull her close and snarl his words.
"By the time I'm done with you,
you'll be begging for the bullet
that coward never shot."

The Nerve

Master's wrong.
I is smart.
I is useful.
And I gots more nerve than anybody I know.

Lips tight,
I raise my head,
I raise the gun,
and set my sights on where they struggle.

My Master and my girl.

And then,

I squeeze.

At Last

I see Shad raise the gun,
but this time
I don't stop him.

This time,
I close my eyes.

Let him shoot, I think.
Maybe it's better to be shot dead
outta love,
than be made live a long life of suffering
outta hate.

The gun explodes in the distance,
echoes in my muffled mind.
And I fall.

Free.
At last.

Black Hole

I open my eyes,
surprised I can,
and roll over to see
Master Duncan,
flat on his back,
staring blind at the wide night sky,
a black hole in his vest,
dripping blood
and seeds.

Shadows

I turn my head, sure I seen something in the woods.
If it ain't paddyrollers,
it soon will be.
Two black slaves
next to two white corpses
is soon dead theyselves.

We gots to get out of here. Me and Shad.

I crawl over to where he lying,
looking up at the night sky.
Only he trickling tears.
"Phoebe!" He take my hand in his. His fingers cold.
"You ain't shot?"

"No, but Master gone."
I wonder which one of us he aimed for.

"We got to go, Shad," I say, kneeling by him.
"If we's—"

according to Phoebe

A rustling in the bushes
stops my words,
stops my heart.

 Too late.

We's already found.

Catching Up

Will and Birdman creep outta the shadows
and onto the moonlit road.
"Davey and Joe hid the wagon ahead," Birdman say.
"Can you make it?"
Like he don't think we can.
Shad and me, we's a sorry sight.
But Shad look between Birdman and Will
and finally see answers.
"I was right about you, Doctor," Shad cough.
"I knew you's up to something."

Birdman check Shad's chest.

"That bag was yours, wasn't it?
You's the abolitionist Master read about in the paper,
ain't you?"
Birdman look over at Master's body.

"He won't hear you ... he dead," Shad say.
"I shot him."

"Shadrach," Will and I kneel by his brother.
"You something else."
Will smile,
but it drop when Birdman meet his eyes
and shake his head.

Will take his brother's hand.

"You came back," Shad whisper.
"Just like Phoebe.
I knew you all wouldn't leave me."

Shad look down at his broken body.
"But ... I think I's just gonna rest here a while.
You go on ahead ...
I'll catch up."
He smile the saddest one I ever seen.

"Oh, Shad," I say, resting my other hand
where his heart
skip and
chug.

All of us knowing it slowing
to a stop.

Sorry

"I'm sorry," Shad say.
"For all I did."
He look at Will.
At me.
"But most of all, I'm sorry
for all I'll never do."

His breath fading now and Shad with it.
And I wonder how such a big soul,
how such a bright spark
can be so easily snuffed.

Shad cough and wheeze,
like it pain him just to breathe,
and I lean in close to hear his whispered words.
"I could have made you happy," he say.
"I could have made you love me."

"You did, Shad."
I squeeze his hand,

even as he let go.

I kiss his lips,

even as he breathe his last.

And I bless his heart,

even as it stop.

"You already did."

Choices

I can't believe he's gone.
Big Will kiss his brother's head
and I know, then, how much it pain him to let him go.
How much he loved Shad.
I hope Shad knew that, too.

"He found your bag," I say. "He hid it to keep you safe."
Will nod, wipe his nose on the back of his hand.
"But I knew you needed it. I knew you needed to be free.
So I took it back and he followed me.
It's my fault Shad here."

"No," Will say. "It ain't.
You made your choices. Just like I made mine.
And Shad made his.
You ain't responsible for what someone else choose.
The only choices you get to make,
the only ones you gots to live with,
is your own.
Shad never understood that."

But I do.

"Well, Phoebe," Birdman say, helping me to my feet
where we stand at the crossroads.
"Looks like you have another choice to make.
There are no witnesses, no survivors, but you.
You can sneak back to your pallet
and no one would be the wiser.
You are free to go back to Whitehaven,
if that's what you want."

"Free to go back?" I say, knowing that caged life
ain't no freedom at all.
And I realized every choice I made:
          collecting words,
                    and secrets,
                              stealing bags
                                        and freeing Yellowbird;
          each choice was like one goose,
that together make a flying v pointing north.
Each choice was one small step
bringing me to where I now stand.
Making it easy to make the next:

"I choose freedom, Birdman," I say.
"I want to go to Canada."

The Road

Will and Phoebe weep for hours,
thinking of the lad left where he lay
on the road behind.

But I'm more concerned about the long road ahead,
for Will, Davey, Joe, and Phoebe.
Fugitive slaves.
A dead master in the mix.
They're bound to be pursued right up to the border,
maybe even into Canada.
If they make it that far.

Many don't.

Hope

We stop at the shore, after many long miles,
much later than I'd planned.
It's almost dawn.
I hope he waited.
Still, I wouldn't blame him if he left.
Patrols roam the river's edge for criminals
bootlegging barrels of booze,
freeing fugitive slaves,
illicit deals of malt and men.
A boat has no business out here in the dark.
No legal business, anyhow.
He risks his life each time. We both do.
But how can we not?

I whistle over the dark waters.
I call again.

And its echo answers, eerie in the misty night.

He's here.

I've never known his name
or his face.
It's safer that way.
Each of us doing what we can
with what we have
for the person God put in our path.
Each of us trusting there is
still good in the world.

Still hope for mankind.

Ohio River

"He'll row you to the other side," I say,
handing Will the bag as the small boat appears,
the familiar form hunched at the oars.

"Cross the river,
let your compass lead you north for three nights,
don't travel by day
and keep off the roads," I say.
Crumbs of advice.
Just enough to lead them safely
to where they can get another handful of help.
Careful not to burden them with more than they can carry.

"Look for the farm with the waterwheel,
the candle in the window.
They'll take you in and tell you where to go next.
I've sent word. They are expecting …
a shipment."

I smile, then.

Shake the men's hands.
Take Phoebe's.

"Good luck, my friends," I say.

Hoping I'll see them again.
Wondering if I will.

Lost

"You ain't coming with us?" I ask.
How we supposed to find our way without Birdman?
The world outside Whitehaven
suddenly seem such a big, dark place
and me lost in it.

"I'm going to Tennessee next," he say.
"More birdwatching.
More bags to deliver.
More shipments to send."
He smile.

And I wonder—
"You ever send a shipment
from the Scott plantation down in Carolina?"
He think for a moment.
"As a matter of fact, I did," he say. "A few years ago.
Four men
and three women."

"Was one called Ruth?" I ask, daring to hope.

Birdman look at me in surprise. "Yes," he say.
"I saw her when I was home last.
She works at the Willard Hotel in St. Catharines."

And I know then where I's going.
Even if I don't yet know the way,
the where,
or the how.

I know one thing:

I ain't lost no more.

Strangers and Friends

The rowboat scrape the shallows
and we go down to meet it.
A man at the oars nods at Birdman.
It time to go.

"Avoid the towns," Birdman say
as he hold it steady for me to climb in.
"Come tomorrow,
you'll be on wanted posters from here to the Falls.
But don't worry. I've been on a few myself
and they haven't caught me yet."

I realize what he done for us;
what Birdman risk,
what Boatman risk,
for strangers.

Birdman give us a shove into the deeper waters.
My heart pounds in my chest.
I don't know how to swim.

I don't know where to run.
I don't know if I can do this.

"*A friend of a friend sent me,*" Birdman say as we pull away.
"That's the password.
It's a long road to freedom
but you've got friends to help you,
and the courage to make it,
step by step."

We drift ahead into the dark unknown,
as Birdman disappear into the shadows behind,
and I think
maybe the world outside Whitehaven
ain't so scary.

Not if there's more people like Birdman in it.

Courage

It takes courage
> to be what the good Lord made you,
> when everyone else
> trying to make you something you ain't.

It takes courage
> to see truths
> that we'd rather not.

It takes courage
> to speak up
> when the way things is,
> ain't the way they should be.

It takes courage
> to go beyond what you know
> to the places you don't.

But you can get there—the promised land.
We all will.

Alls we need is the courage
to take one step at a time.

And that's the gospel truth.

Acknowledgements:

Thanks so much to:
Peter Carver for giving me the freedom to find this story and the courage to tell it. Your mentorship has helped me find my voice and follow my dream.

Richard Dionne and the Red Deer team for your continuous support and hard work.

Marie Campbell for your steadfast support and encouragement, particularly when I needed it most.

A heartfelt thanks to:
Alan Cranny for capturing the spirit of the novel in the cover art.

Kerri Chartrand, Tony Pignat, Fiona Jackson, Alan Cranny, and Peggy Cranny for reading draft after draft.

Tony, Liam, and Marion for all you do and all you are. May you always have wisdom to know your truth and the courage to speak it.

Photo credit: Tony Pignat

Interview with Caroline Pignat

What drew you to this time and place?

This was supposed to be the fourth and final book in the *Greener Grass* series—Annie's story. As I was researching her time period, I learned about the Fugitive Slave Act of 1850. By the 1850s, slavery had been a part of life in the southern United States for over 200 years. It was simply the way of things, passed on from one generation to the next. Slaves were bought and bred to work the land (usually cotton, sugar, or tobacco crops) and serve the master. They had no rights or freedoms. In fact, in most southern states, anyone caught teaching a slave to read would be fined, imprisoned, or whipped.

For as long as there has been slavery, there have been those who tried to escape from it. But those numbers increased with The Fugitive Slave Act of 1850 [enacted by the U.S. Congress], which stated that any runaway slaves must be returned to their masters and that anyone who helped the fugitives would also be punished. This law stated that anyone in the United States who helped runaway slaves escape could be fined or arrested. It also gave the U.S. federal marshal the power to deputize and enlist whomever he wanted, to assist in the capture of fugitive slaves (whether they wanted to help or not.) The Fugitive Slave Act meant there was no safe place for fugitive slaves to live in the United States, and there are instances of free men being caught and returned south. It's not surprising so many people looked north to Canada for equality and freedom. In fact, just one month after that law was passed, over 3,000 African-Americans made their way to Canada, and between 1840 and 1860 more than 30,000 American slaves came to Canada.

I started to write the story from Annie's point of view—maybe she was an abolitionist or maybe she worked for one. But as I learned more, I became intrigued by the injustice of slavery and especially by the courage it would have taken a slave to even think of running away from all he or she knows. That's when I started to write in Phoebe's voice and when I realized this was her story, not Annie's.

What gave you the confidence to write in this voice?

Who am I to write this story? Good question. In writing *Greener Grass*, I had roots and relatives. I was an Irish immigrant. I felt some ownership of the story I told. Some right to that voice—my main character did, after all, sound just like my Granny.

But I hesitated when the idea for *The Gospel Truth* became clearer. After all, who am I—a white, suburban, middle-class mom—to write this story?

Was it even mine to tell?

Unlike my other novels, this was not my journey, not my heritage, not my voice—and yet it fascinated me. I'll do the research, I told myself, and see. I soon realized this journey wasn't about telling a story as much as it was about listening to others'.

How did you develop such an authentic voice for these characters?

I listened to them. If you want to understand anyone, past or present, you've got to be willing to listen to their stories.

In any research, primary sources are key. Imagine being able to hear what it was really like from someone who has been there. Sometimes you can find those voices in old newspaper articles, letters, or journals. But since it was considered unnecessary and often illegal for slaves to read or write (in fact, you could get charged for teaching them) I wondered if first hand accounts might be difficult to find.

Thankfully, The Library of Congress has a collection of over 2,000 interviews with former slaves that are transcribed as spoken. Here's one example:

None of us was 'lowed to see a book or try to learn. Dey say we git smarter den dey was if we learn anything, but we slips around and gits hold of dat Webster's old blue black speller and we hides it 'til way in de night and den we lights a little pine torch and studies dat spellin' book. We learn it too.

—Jenny Proctor, *Unchained Memories*

Unchained Memories is a book/DVD that shares photos and excerpts from those narratives that gave vivid details about slave life. It felt like I was interviewing hundreds of former slaves.

I also read sources like *Narratives of Fugitive Slaves in Canada* by Benjamin Drew and autobiographies like *Incidents in the Life of a Slave Girl* by Harriet Jacobs, *Twelve Years a Slave* by Solomon Northrop and *The Life of Josiah Henson* by Josiah Henson. It fascinated me to see their world through their eyes.

All of these testimonies were so compelling and I realized that though each individual experienced slavery, their stories and worldview differed. That was why even brothers like Shad and Will don't see things the same. It was why some slaves ran and others stayed. All of that primary source material was integral to developing a vivid and varied sense of voice.

Why is it important to tell this story today?

Narratives, biographies, abolitionists' writings, and research of that time and place, helped me imagine what it must be like to walk in their shoes, to see their world, their truths through their eyes. We start to understand and even relate—and empathy grows.

From time to time, we need to quiet that familiar voice of our own so we can hear the truth of another's. We need to see things from new perspectives to better inform our own. I will never claim to have a right to this story, but I do have a duty to it. We all do. To listen. To learn. To see and to share.

Imagine what life would have been like back then if they approached each other with that same empathy.

Imagine what it would be like today if we all did.

Some would say that writing a story about escaping slaves runs the danger of focusing on African Americans as victims—a common enough portrayal. In what way do you think Phoebe, Bea, Will and other slaves are not victims?

To me, victims are "defeated." As a result of all they've suffered, they've succumbed and given up hope. What moved me the most in my research was the strength and resilience of the human spirit. Despite unspeakable injustices and suffering, so many of those voices spoke with unwavering hope. Like many slaves, Phoebe, Bea, and Will were scarred inside and out, but they held on to their hopes and dreams. Even when their world, their master, and the law told them otherwise, they believed in what they knew to be true.

One of the main characters in the story is Dr. Bergman—who is based on a real historical figure, Dr. Alexander Ross, a Canadian. Why is Dr. Ross such an important figure in the history of the Underground Railroad?

The Underground Railroad was a complex network of people, men and women, black and white, American and Canadian who worked together to help slaves escape to freedom. It was "underground" because their actions were considered illegal in the South; they were "stealing property," after all.

Dr. Alexander Milton Ross, a Canadian abolitionist, posed as an ornithologist while visiting Southern plantations. Under the guise of birdwatching, "the Birdman" secretly met with enslaved people and give them information and a few supplies to help them start their journey. In his Underground Railroad role as "ticket agent," he'd make arrangements for them to meet "conductors," people who, like Harriet Tubman, played key roles in helping fugitive slaves move from one "station" or safe house to the next. It was dangerous work for all involved. Dr. Ross had several warrants for his arrest and generous rewards were offered to anyone who might turn him in.

Phoebe's mother tells her about the birds in her world. How much research did you have to do on birds and bird calls as you were writing this story?

When I was nine, I started at a new school in a new country (my family had moved from Canada to Ireland). I missed my old home, the life I'd left and especially my friends. I remember it being a tough transition for me and a very lonely time. Sister Killian, my Grade 3 teacher at my new school, was an avid birdwatcher and her enthusiasm for it was contagious. Thanks to her, I too became as passionate and though I knew nothing about the names or species, watching flocks swoop, gulls soar, or finding an old nest brought me such joy. It still does. Today, a favorite place of mine is a nearby nature trail where, if you're quiet enough and still enough, the chickadees perch on your pinky and eat seed from your outstretched hand. It amazes me every time.

For the novel, I did research about the birds of Virginia, nesting habits, bird calls—and I read a fascinating book called *What the Robin Knows* by Jon Young that looks at the secret language of nature conveyed through bird behavior and vocalization. Like me, Phoebe might not know the birds' scientific names or species—but she knew their secret language. She learned from their wisdom. I think we all do, if we are still enough to listen.

Some see the writer as someone who likes to explore and capture the themes and characters and events that come out of her own experience. But you have gone beyond your comfort zone with this story. What were the rewards for you in doing that?

Writing this novel was an unnerving experience for a lot of reasons. First of all, as I mentioned earlier, the voice was completely new.

Secondly, there was the unusual form. Writing in first person is like being inside your character's head—and writing in free verse is like being inside your character's heart. It's powerful, raw, and resonates when done well. I knew when I wrote the poems in *Egghead* that someday I wanted to try a whole novel in free verse, but the process really surprised me. Actually, for a control freak like me, it was terrifying. Instead of moving from one plot point to the next, like the highly structured dot-to-dot plotting of my other novels, free verse is messy, organic, and at times, uncontrollable. It's like the fingerpainting or the watercolors of writing. It pushed me outside the lines, way outside my comfort zone, and forced me to let go. Just play, just create, it said, and see what happens. Yes, it was terrifying and exhilarating, but I think we end up with the most spontaneous, vibrant, and completely unique pieces of art that way.

The third risky move was to attempt to write a free verse novel in six voices. I needed to know each of the six characters as well as I knew Phoebe. Also, each voice needed to be unique and consistent and, in terms of plot, I needed to ensure I wove the six threads logically. Who was the best person to witness and tell that particular part of the story?

The reward of going beyond what is safe and familiar, as scary as that may be, is discovering new worlds and perspectives. Phoebe learns that in this novel—and so did I.

Most of the books you have written are historical novels. What is it about this genre that interests you and that you think interests young readers?

I've always loved reading historical fiction and writing it is even more intriguing. Not only do the characters deal with the struggles we all have in everyday life, but on top of that they are caught up in an incredible moment in history. Famine and fever. Shipwrecks or slavery. Each historical event provides huge external conflicts that stir up great inner turmoil. In that way, the history not only determines the setting and enriches the plot, it also shapes the characters.

When my students tell me they don't like reading, I say that's like saying you don't like eating. We are wired for story. We need it, just like food. The trick is to keep sampling until you find your favorite because without it, your soul would certainly starve.

In the end, everyone loves a great story—and history is loaded with them.

Thank you, Caroline, for your thoughtful insights into the life of a writer.